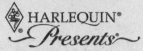

Welcome to this month's books from Harlequin
Presents! The fabulously passionate series
THE ROYAL HOUSE OF NIROLI continues with
The Tycoon's Princess Bride by Natasha Oakley,
where Princess Isabella Fierezza risks forfeiting
her chance to be queen when she falls for
Niroli's enemy, Domenic Vincini. And don't miss
The Spanish Prince's Virgin Bride, the final part of
Sandra Marton's trilogy THE BILLIONAIRES' BRIDES,
in which Prince Lucas Reyes believes his contract fiancée
is pretending she's never been touched by another man!

Also this month, favorite author Helen Bianchin brings
you *The Greek Tycoon's Virgin Wife,* where gorgeous
Xandro Caramanis wants a wife—and an heir. In
Innocent on Her Wedding Night by Sara Craven,
Daniel meets his estranged wife again—and wants
to claim the wedding night that was never his. In
The Boss's Wife for a Week by Anne McAllister,
Spence Tyack's assistant Sadie proves not only to be
sensible in the boardroom, but also sensual in the
bedroom! In *The Mediterranean Billionaire's Secret
Baby* by Diana Hamilton, Italian billionaire Francesco
Mastroianni is shocked to see his ex-mistress again after
seven months—and she's visibly pregnant! In *Willingly
Bedded, Forcibly Wedded* by Melanie Milburne,
Jasper Caulfield has to marry Hayley or he'll lose his
inheritance. But she's determined to be a wife on paper
only. Finally brilliant new author India Grey brings you
her first book, *The Italian's Defiant Mistress,* where
only millionaire Raphael di Lazaro can help Eve—if she
becomes his mistress....

Men who can't be tamed...or so they think!

If you love strong, commanding men, you'll love this miniseries.

Meet the guy who breaks the rules to get exactly what he wants, because he is...

HARD-EDGED & HANDSOME
He's the man who's impossible to resist.

RICH & RAKISH
He's got everything—and needs nobody... until he meets one woman.

He's RUTHLESS!
In his pursuit of passion. In his world the winner takes all!

Brought to you by your favorite Harlequin Presents® authors!

Sara Craven

INNOCENT ON HER WEDDING NIGHT

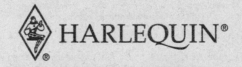

TORONTO • NEW YORK • LONDON
AMSTERDAM • PARIS • SYDNEY • HAMBURG
STOCKHOLM • ATHENS • TOKYO • MILAN • MADRID
PRAGUE • WARSAW • BUDAPEST • AUCKLAND

If you purchased this book without a cover you should be aware
that this book is stolen property. It was reported as "unsold and
destroyed" to the publisher, and neither the author nor the
publisher has received any payment for this "stripped book."

ISBN-13: 978-0-373-12670-5
ISBN-10:   0-373-12670-0

INNOCENT ON HER WEDDING NIGHT

First North American Publication 2007.

Copyright © 2007 by Sara Craven.

All rights reserved. Except for use in any review, the reproduction or
utilization of this work in whole or in part in any form by any electronic,
mechanical or other means, now known or hereafter invented, including
xerography, photocopying and recording, or in any information storage
or retrieval system, is forbidden without the written permission of the
publisher, Harlequin Enterprises Limited, 225 Duncan Mill Road,
Don Mills, Ontario, Canada M3B 3K9.

This is a work of fiction. Names, characters, places and incidents are
either the product of the author's imagination or are used fictitiously,
and any resemblance to actual persons, living or dead, business
establishments, events or locales is entirely coincidental.

This edition published by arrangement with Harlequin Books S.A.

® and TM are trademarks of the publisher. Trademarks indicated with
® are registered in the United States Patent and Trademark Office, the
Canadian Trade Marks Office and in other countries.

www.eHarlequin.com

Printed in U.S.A.

All about the author...
Sara Craven

SARA CRAVEN was born in south Devon, England, and grew up surrounded by books in a house by the sea. After leaving grammar school she worked as a local journalist, covering everything from flower shows to murders. She started writing for Harlequin Books in 1975. Sara has appeared as a contestant on the U.K. Channel Four game show *Fifteen to One*, and in 1997 won the title of Television Mastermind of Great Britain.

Sara shares her Somerset home with a West Highland white terrier called Bertie Wooster, several thousand books and an amazing video and DVD collection.

When she's not writing, she likes to travel in Europe, particularly in Greece and Italy. She loves music, theater, cooking and eating in good restaurants, but reading will always be her greatest passion.

Since the birth of her twin grandchildren in New York City, she has become a regular visitor to the Big Apple.

CHAPTER ONE

As THE lift began its journey to the fourth floor, Laine Sinclair put down her bulky travel bag, flexing cramped fingers, and sagged back against the metal wall.

Adrenalin had got her this far, fuelled largely by anger and disappointment, but now, with sanctuary almost within reach, the savage energy was draining out of her, reminding her that she was jet-lagged and that her damaged ankle, in spite of its rudimentary bandaging, hurt like hell.

Home, she thought longingly, raking a hand through her light sun-streaked hair. Home, bath—and bed. Especially bed. Maybe she'd wait long enough to make herself a hot drink. Probably she wouldn't.

There'd be no one around at the flat. Jamie would be at work, and it wasn't one of the cleaner's days. So there'd be no cosseting, however much she might need it.

But there would be absolute peace and quiet, and the opportunity to sleep off some of her stresses and strains before the inquisition started.

She could hear it now. *What are you doing back here? What happened to the boat charter business? And where's Andy?*

At some point she would have to come up with the answers to all that, and more, but she'd worry about that when she had to. And that, she thought, was not yet.

And at least Jamie, with his own chequered career, was unlikely to say *I told you so*.

The lift stopped, and as the doors slid open she hefted her bag on to her shoulder, and stepped into the corridor, wincing as her ankle protested.

She fumbled in her travel belt for her latch key. She hadn't intended to take it with her. It was to have been left behind, like a symbol of her old life.

Not needed on voyage, she thought, her mouth twisting. And how ironic was that?

She let herself in, put down her bag, and stood, looking appraisingly around her at the big living room which, with the galley kitchen opposite her, formed the flat's neutral territory. Two *en-suite* bedrooms faced each other across the shared space, ruled by their own strict privacy laws. A system that worked, and generally worked well.

She noted, brows raised, that the flat seemed unusually tidy for once, with none of the empty wine bottles, crumpled newspapers and takeaway cartons that marked her brother's normal passage through life when she wasn't there to prevent it.

Maybe all that persistent nagging had paid off at last. And at least she wouldn't have to clear a path to get to her own immaculate bedroom.

But on that thought dawned two others. First—that the door to her room was standing open, when it should be closed. Secondly—that she could hear someone moving around inside.

Well, what do I know? she thought wearily. I haven't been here for over a month. Maybe Mrs Archer's changed her hours, and that's why the place is almost hygienic for once.

Her lips parted to call out—to establish her presence and reassure—but the words were never uttered. Instead, her bedroom door was flung wide, and a stark naked man walked out into the living room.

Laine shrieked. Closing her eyes, she took a too-hasty step backwards and stumbled against her abandoned bag, ricking her

ankle again, and sending a shaft of pain up her leg which made
her teeth ache in sympathy.

The interloper said something that combined blasphemy and
obscenity in one gracefully drawled phrase, then vanished back
into the room he'd just left.

Leaving Laine standing there as if she'd been turned to stone,
a small frightened voice in her head whispering a beseeching
No—oh, no…over and over again.

Because she knew that voice. Knew it as well as she knew her
own, even though she'd never expected to hear it again.

The body she hadn't recognised from that brief glimpse, but
then she'd never seen it less than partially clothed before.

However, she was in no doubt at all over the intruder's
identity. In which case, she thought shakily, grabbing at her bag,
she was on her way out of here.

She was halfway to the door when she heard his voice again,
reaching her across the room.

'Elaine.' The hated full version of her name, pronounced with
a kind of weary disdain. 'Of all the people in the world. What
the *hell* are you doing here?'

'*Daniel?*' Somehow she made herself say it. Utter it aloud.
'Daniel—Flynn?'

She turned back slowly and carefully, dry-mouthed, noting
with relief that at least he had a towel draped round his hips this
time, as he stood in her bedroom doorway, one bare shoulder
propped almost negligently against its frame.

He hadn't changed much in the past two years, she thought
numbly. Not on the surface, anyway. The unruly dark hair,
shining with damp, was still longer than convention demanded.
The lean, incisive face with its high cheekbones and sculpted
mouth, was as heart-stopping as ever. The tall body was even
more powerful than she remembered, with the long endless legs,
and the deep shadow of chest hair that arrowed down towards
his flat stomach.

So, although the rudimentary decencies had been observed,

there was still clearly nothing to be relieved about, she told herself as she began to shake inside. In fact, quite the contrary...

'I don't believe it.' She invested her tone with considered venom. 'My God, I hoped I'd seen the last of you.'

'And instead you saw a damned sight more than you bargained for.' He looked her up and down, the hazel eyes frankly insolent under their heavy fringe of lashes as he took in the grubby white denims, and crumpled dark blue top. 'That's life?'

'What are you doing here?' Laine lifted her chin haughtily, trying not to blush.

'Taking a shower.' His tanned face was inimical. 'Isn't it obvious?'

'And equally obvious that isn't what I meant.' She struggled to steady her voice. To try and regain some control of this disturbing and unwelcome situation. 'I'm asking what you're doing in this flat.'

'But I asked first,' he said. 'I understood you were establishing a new career being decorative in the Florida Keys.'

'I was working in a boat charter business down there, yes,' she said curtly. 'What's it to you?'

'I was simply wondering why you're stumbling around here instead of fixing frozen daiquiris on the poop deck.'

'I don't have to explain myself to you,' Laine said coldly. 'All you need to know is that I'm home to stay, and you can get dressed and the hell out of my flat before I have the law on you.'

His look was contemptuous. 'And I'm supposed to tremble and obey? Is that it? No chance, sweetness. Because, unless your dear brother's been lying to me, and frankly I don't think he'd dare, half this desirable residence is his, and that's the half I'm using.'

'*You* are using?' she said slowly. 'By what right?'

'I have a three-month lease,' he said. 'Properly drawn up and legally enforceable.'

Her heart was thudding unevenly against her ribcage. 'I gave no permission for this.'

'You weren't here,' he reminded her. 'And Jamie guaranteed

that happy state of affairs would continue. He thought that you and your fellow boat charterer were all set to walk into the sunset together.' He inspected her bare left hand, his mouth twisting. 'Or did he get that wrong?'

Yes, she thought. Completely wrong. But at the time it had made more sense to let Jamie believe that...

Aloud, she said, 'A slight change of plan.'

'Ah,' he said. 'So another one bit the dust? I do hope you're not making a habit of it.' He waited for the sharp indrawn breath she could not control, then went on smoothly, 'However, it was on the strict understanding that I'd have the place to myself that I arranged to tenant the flat during your brother's absence in the United States.'

'Absence?' she repeated numbly. 'Since when?'

'Since three weeks.' He paused. 'It's a—temporary secondment.'

'Why didn't he let me know?'

'It all happened rather quickly.' The silky drawl was even more pronounced. 'He tried to contact you, but you seemed—unavailable. Phone calls and faxes to your registered office were left unanswered.' He shrugged, drawing her unwilling attention to his elegantly muscled shoulders, and rather more besides.

God, but that towel was skimpy, she thought, her throat tightening. And none too secure either.

She decided to avert her gaze. 'Always supposing this dubious agreement is valid,' she said through gritted teeth, 'that doesn't explain why you were coming out of my bedroom.'

'Except that it's now mine,' he said. 'For the duration.' His smile was harsh. 'I'm sleeping in your bed at last, darling. Now, there's a thought to savour.'

'Not,' she said, 'as far as I'm concerned.'

'There was a time,' he said softly, 'when the idea seemed briefly to hold a certain amount of appeal for you.'

'But that,' she said, 'was before I turned out to be "a cheat, a liar and a bitch". And I quote.'

His brows lifted. 'Indeed you do—and with remarkable accuracy. But moving into your room wasn't a deliberate choice prompted by malice. Or any nostalgia for what might have been,' he added, his mouth curling. 'Simply a question of expediency.'

'However, you must be able to understand,' she went on, as if he hadn't spoken, 'why I wouldn't wish to share a roof with you now any more than I did two years ago.'

'I can see it might be a problem,' he agreed.

'I'm glad you're prepared to be reasonable.' She was surprised, too, she thought, taking another, more even breath. 'Then perhaps you'd make immediate arrangements to remove yourself and your belongings to a more appropriate environment?'

His grin was total appreciation. 'Presumably somewhere like the lowest pit of hell? But you misunderstand me, sweetheart. Any problem that might exist is yours, not mine, because I'm going nowhere. What you decide, of course,' he added, 'is entirely your own business.'

She stared at him, lips parting in dismay. 'But you can't do this.'

He shrugged again, casually adjusting the slipping towel. 'Try me.'

'But you don't really want to live here,' she said uncertainly.

'Why not? Apart from the last five minutes, it's been pleasant enough.'

'But such a come down.' She made herself drawl the words, as if she'd suddenly seen the humour in the situation. 'It's just a flat, after all. Not a glamorous penthouse pad for a millionaire publishing tycoon. No diamond encrusted taps or wall-to-wall women. Not your sort of place at all.'

She paused. 'Unless, of course, Wordwide International has gone into liquidation since you've been running it, and this is all you can afford these days.'

'Sorry to disappoint you,' he said, his face expressionless. 'But things are just fine in our part of the market. And I'm staying here because it's temporarily convenient for me to do so.'

He folded his arms across his chest. 'Face it, Laine, you chose to return without a word to anyone, least of all Jamie. He seemed to think you wouldn't be coming back at all—ever. And life doesn't stand still waiting for you. However, my deal is strictly with Jamie, so I have no power to prevent you using the other half of the flat, if you wish,' he added evenly.

'That's quite impossible.' She didn't look at him. 'And you know it.'

'Actually, no,' he said. 'I don't. Stay—go—it makes no difference to me. Unless you're deluding yourself that I still harbour some faint inclination for you. If so, think again.'

He paused grimly, watching the helpless colour warm her face. 'But be aware of this—you're not going to insult me out of occupation, and an appeal to my better nature won't work either.'

'I wasn't aware you had a better nature.'

'It's currently under severe pressure.' He paused. 'If you won't share, you leave. It's that simple, so make your mind up.'

'This is my home,' she said. 'I have nowhere else to go.'

'Then do what I did,' he said. 'Call in a favour.' He added with a touch of grimness, 'Although I suspect that might be difficult. You and your brother probably owe far more goodwill than you can ever repay.'

Laine drew a swift, sharp breath. 'That is a—loathsome thing to say.'

'But realistic.' He gave her a level look. 'So, if you've finally decided that here is better than a corner of Cardboard City, I suggest you stop arguing and start getting organised, because it could be a lengthy business.

'And if you want to eat, you'll also have to shop, because I'm not funding your food. We'll discuss sharing the other bills later.'

He turned to go. 'And don't ask for your room back,' he added. 'As a refusal often offends.'

'I wouldn't dream of it,' Laine said between her teeth. 'After all, in a few weeks you'll be gone, and until that happy day I'll camp in Jamie's room.'

His grin was sardonic. 'Prior to having this place fumigated and the bed ritually burned, no doubt.'

'My own thoughts precisely,' she threw after him as the door closed.

For a moment she stood where she was, staring at the wooden panels. It's a nightmare, she told herself. That's all. And presently I'll wake up to find it's over, and then I can start putting my life back together again.

She was trembling so violently inside that all she wanted to do was let herself sink down on to the floor and stay there. But Daniel could re-emerge at any moment, and the last thing she wanted was to be found crouching on the stripped and polished floorboards at his feet like some small wounded animal.

She'd never thought she would see him again. Or not face to face like this, anyway. Had told herself that he was out of her life for always. Deliberately put herself at such a distance that she would be spared the pain of even an accidental glimpse of him. Promised herself that, gradually, the memories of everything that had happened between them would begin to fade, and she would find some kind of peace.

Yet here he was again, and all the shame and the trauma of their shared past were still as vivid and as painful as ever.

I haven't forgotten a thing, she thought. And neither has he.

She passed the tip of her tongue over her dry lips. *Faint inclination.* That was the phrase he'd used, and it had bitten into her consciousness like acid dripping on metal.

Because that was as much as it had ever been. All the helpless passion—the feverish longing—had been on her side alone.

But I can't let him think it still matters to me, she told herself. I dare not. I have to convince him that it's all over for me too. That I've grown up and moved on.

She waited until her heartbeat had steadied, and her breathing rate had calmed a little, then made her way slowly over to Jamie's room, favouring her damaged ankle as she went.

She turned the handle and made to push the door open, but it resisted stubbornly, as if there was some obstruction behind it. Laine put her shoulder to it, managing to create a gap just wide enough to give her access, and squeezed through it, wincing.

Then stopped dead, with a gasp of sheer dismay.

Because this was no longer a bedroom, but a landfill site. Every inch of space seemed to be occupied by something. There were stacks of boxes on the floor, next to crates of books and CDs, and a row of suitcases, elderly and unmatching. The bed's bare mattress, she saw incredulously, was covered by the entire contents of her own wardrobe. And the blockage behind the door had been caused by an over-stuffed black binliner which had apparently fallen from a similar pile.

As if in a dream, Laine reached down and lifted it back into place.

Cardboard City, she thought, was right here, waiting for her.

It would take hours, she realised limply, to clear sufficient space just to cross the room. As for the leisurely bath and so-needed sleep—well, that was going to remain just a dream for the foreseeable future.

To her horror, she felt her eyes burning with sudden tears. After all the ghastliness with Andy, to come home to this! Plus *bloody* Daniel Flynn.

A lengthy business. His own words—the rotten bastard.

Because he'd known exactly what she was going to find here. These things weren't Jamie's, so they had to be his. He was sleeping in her room, and using this as his private dumping ground.

'If I could only get to the window,' she muttered furiously, crushing down any lingering remnants of self-pity. 'I'd throw the whole sodding lot into the street.'

He'd emptied everything she possessed on to the bed—even her underwear—and the thought made her cringe. She'd wash and iron every single item before she allowed any of them anywhere near her, she promised herself grimly.

But if he thought she was going to deal with this appalling mess alone, he could think again. He was *not* going to get away with it, she vowed as she limped back across the living room and banged on the door.

It was flung open almost immediately, and Daniel confronted her unsmilingly. The towel had been replaced by a pair of jeans, but he was still barefoot and bare-chested, and Laine felt her mouth dry as unwanted memory pierced her.

'What now?' he demanded.

'That other room,' she said huskily, 'is a pigsty. A tip. And I want to know what you intend to do about it.'

'Nothing,' he returned curtly. 'Not my tip. Not my problem.'

Laine gasped. 'What the hell do you mean? It's packed to the ceiling with your surplus belongings, and I want them moved. Now.'

'The true voice of command.' His mouth curled. 'Your sea-faring days haven't been wasted. What's next on the agenda, Captain? A little light keel-hauling?'

She jerked a thumb in the direction of the room behind her. 'That is now my half of the flat,' she said. 'And I want it cleared.'

'Then I suggest you get started.' He sounded faintly bored. 'Although God knows where you're going to put it all. And—just for the record—nothing in that room is mine. Some of the things belong to your brother, but most of it he's storing for someone called Sandra. I believe she went with him to New York.'

'Jamie left them?' She stared at him. 'Left me to cope with that terrible mess? Oh, he couldn't have done. He wouldn't...' Her voice trailed away.

'No?' His smile was cynical. 'If you wish to take the matter up with him, I can give you his number in Manhattan.'

'Please don't trouble yourself,' she said crisply. 'I'll manage.'

She'd planned to wheel round and march away with dignity, but in mid-turn her ankle gave a jab of pain so fierce that she yelped aloud and faltered.

'Going for the sympathy vote, Laine? It won't work.'

But neither would her ankle, she realised, taking a deep breath as she gingerly tested her weight on it and winced uncontrollably.

'What's the matter?' One swift stride brought him to her, his hand under her elbow.

'Don't touch me.' She tried to pull away, but he'd seen the bandage and his grip tightened.

'What the hell have you done to yourself?' He sounded resigned.

'My ankle's twisted, that's all,' she said shortly. 'Please leave me alone, and don't fuss.'

'I'm not the one squawking with pain.'

To her horror, Daniel picked her up and carried her to one of the long sofas that flanked the fireplace, placing her on the cushions. It was the work of a moment, but it forced an all-too potent reminder of the cool, clean scent of his bare skin into her consciousness.

Oh, God, she thought, a feeling akin to panic unravelling inside her, I don't need this…

He knelt, and began to undo the bandage.

She said tautly, 'I can manage by myself.'

His glance was ironic. 'Now who's making the fuss?'

Laine subsided, flushing mutinously. She stared over his shoulder, her teeth sinking into her lower lip, her nerve-endings jangling as Daniel frowningly examined the swollen joint.

'When did you do this?'

She hunched a shoulder. 'The other day.'

'You should have rested it at once,' he said tersely. 'So start now.' He rose lithely and went into the kitchen, returning a few minutes later with a plastic bag filled with ice cubes. 'Here. Hold this against it.'

She complied reluctantly, her expression rebellious as Daniel tied it on with the discarded bandage.

'Thank you,' she said tautly when his task was completed.

'No need for gratitude,' he said caustically as he straightened. 'I have a vested interest in seeing that you have both legs in good working order. Job hunting requires a lot of exercise, and you need to start earning without delay.'

She lifted her chin. 'Please don't worry. I've always paid my way.'

'Not always,' he said softly. 'But these days I prefer cash, rather than kind. It's more reliable.'

She was rigid. 'What is that supposed to mean?'

'Work it out for yourself,' he said coldly, and disappeared back to the kitchen, leaving her gasping in fury. When he returned, he was carrying a glass of water on a saucer, with two capsules lying beside it.

'Here,' he said. 'Take these.'

'What are they?'

'Painkillers,' he said with a hint of acid. 'Don't worry. You won't wake up in two days' time in some Middle Eastern brothel.'

If you knew, she thought, as she reluctantly swallowed the capsules, and handed back the glass. If you had the least idea of what's happened in the past few days, then perhaps you'd understand why I'm strung on wires. But you don't—and anyway you're the last person in the world that I could ever tell.

He was looking at her frowningly. 'Have you eaten?'

'There was food on the plane,' she returned evasively. She hadn't touched any of it. She'd felt sick to her stomach, as well as sick at heart, her mind going in dazed circles as she tried to make sense of what Andy had done. The brutal extent of his betrayal.

And to come reeling out of hell, after all she'd been through, to find this man of all men waiting for her was the final shattering blow.

He paused. 'I'm going to make coffee. Do you want some?'

Laine shook her head. 'No—thank you.'

She leaned back against the cushions, closing her eyes. Blocking him out physically would be a start, she thought wearily. The beginning of a long, uphill struggle to free herself from him, and the memories he evoked, which, incredibly, still had the power to devastate even two long years further on.

But her senses still told her when he moved away, and how pathetic was that? How could she be so aware of a man who'd deliberately and cynically betrayed her? Who'd destroyed her self-esteem and her trust, along with the first delirious ache of first love. A love that had left her in small pieces, unfulfilled and almost destroyed:

But she couldn't let herself think about that. Not now. Not ever. She had other far more important considerations to deal with—like finding work.

As he'd so charmingly indicated, she thought, gritting her teeth.

She could hear the distant chink of crockery as he moved around in the kitchen, and shifted restlessly on the cushions.

Oh, God, these coming weeks were going to be the kind of agony that no painkillers could ever touch, but, whatever her feelings, she couldn't afford to move out immediately, and he probably knew it.

She'd always hoped that if they ever met again by some mischance, far in the future, she'd be so bolstered by her own success—her own happiness—that she could look him in the eye with indifference.

But Fate had planned it otherwise.

She had no idea how much money she had in her bank account, but it couldn't be much. And she'd used the last remaining bit of credit on her card to buy her ticket home, so that was another bill she could expect eventually.

And now, with Jamie gone, she couldn't even beg a temporary loan.

I think I've just hit rock bottom, she thought. Unless there's another layer they haven't mentioned.

'Don't go to sleep, Laine.' His voice made her jump. 'Try and switch yourself to London time, or you could be jet-lagged for days.'

She opened reluctant eyes and looked at him. He was holding out a beaker.

'I suggest you drink this. You need the caffeine to get you started.'

She said haughtily, 'If this is intended as some kind of olive branch…'

'I know. I can stick it where the sun don't shine. But don't worry. It's not peace I'm offering—more an armed truce. Now, take it.'

She bit her lip, and obeyed with open reluctance. The brew it contained was black and strong without sugar, just as she liked it, which somehow made acceptance even more galling.

He sat down on the sofa opposite, stretching out long legs, observing her narrow-eyed. 'And what are your career plans now that boat chartering has hit the rocks?'

She stiffened defensively. 'I didn't actually say that.'

'You didn't have to. You hardly came in whistling *A life on the ocean wave.*'

She took another sip of coffee while she tried to think of an acceptable approximation of the truth. 'Let's just say that my partner and I discovered we had irreconcilable differences and leave it at that.'

Daniel's brows lifted sardonically. 'Well, that has a familiar ring,' he commented, making her wince inwardly. 'Is this a final breach, or more of a decree nisi?'

'What do you mean?'

'Is it over, or only over unless—or until—he comes grovelling on his knees for forgiveness?'

Her stomach gave a sudden crazy lurch. 'That won't happen. And I'd rather not discuss it any further.'

'A Sinclair family trait,' he said softly. 'Leaving all kinds of things unsaid. Rather like trying to cap a volcano, don't you think?'

'No,' she said stonily. 'I don't. I think privacy should be respected.'

'Is that why you couldn't be reached in Florida?'

No, she thought. That was because Andy hadn't paid the rent on our office, and the landlord closed it down. But I didn't know that at the time.

'Jamie and I are brother and sister,' she returned. 'But we're not joined at the hip.'

'I can tell that,' he said. 'Sandra came as quite a surprise, didn't she?'

'Jamie's had a lot of girls, and will probably have many more,' she said. 'It's no big deal.'

'I think,' he said, 'this one might be.'

'Oh, really?' Her tone was sarcastic. 'You've been out of our lives for two years. Now you're suddenly in my brother's confidence? I don't think so.'

'You're the one that's out of touch, Laine. Jamie and I have been in contact quite a lot in recent months—one way and another.'

There was something about that—the phrasing, perhaps, or an odd note in his voice—which sent a prickle of unease down her spine.

Because on the face of it there was no need, or even likelihood, for their paths to cross. Jamie was a minor cog in a firm of City accountants. Daniel had inherited his family business empire and become a publishing magnate before he was thirty.

And, besides, he'd been Simon's friend, she thought flatly, fighting the instinctive pain. No one else's. Simon, her adored eldest brother, the golden boy, ten years her senior.

Daniel's best mate at school from way back. Both high-flyers in the sixth form, members of the First Eleven at cricket, and demon tennis partners.

But there the resemblance ended. Because Daniel was a loner, the only son of a driven father who, after his wife's death, had poured all his energies, all his emotions into work, into relentless expansion and acquisition, leaving little time to give to a small boy. In school holidays he'd been left to the mercies of paid staff, or farmed out to various business acquaintances with young families.

While Simon had had his mother, two younger siblings, and Abbotsbrook, that wonderful crumbling relic of a house with its huge untidy garden to come home to at the end of each term. A place where every summer gave the illusion of being filled with sun and warmth.

Eventually, grudgingly, Robert Flynn had agreed that his son could spend part of his holidays with his friend's family.

After all, as Angela Sinclair had remarked, the house was always full of people. There were guests almost every weekend. One more would make little difference.

Except to me, Laine thought with a pang. It made all the difference in the world to me…

But that was forbidden territory, and she dared not go there. Particularly now.

She finished her coffee, and put the beaker on the floor. 'Jamie's well below your league, isn't he? You always seemed to regard him as something of a pain. And you certainly can't be short of places to live, so why here?'

'It's an arrangement that suited us both.'

'And Cowper Dymond don't have a New York branch,' she went on. 'So what's Jamie doing over there?'

'He's working for me,' Daniel said. 'In the royalties section of Hirondelle Books.'

'Working for you?' Laine's voice was incredulous, but her uneasy feeling grew. 'But he had a perfectly good job. Why should he change?'

'Perhaps that's something else you should discuss with him?' Daniel drained his coffee cup and rose. 'He's expecting your call.'

She stared up at him. 'You've been talking to him? You told him I was here?'

'While I was in the kitchen,' he said. 'I suggested that his room should be cleared, and the contents put into storage at his expense, and he agreed. Unfortunately, the removal firm I called can't come until tomorrow, so you may have to spend the night on that sofa.'

'*You* called?' Laine lifted her chin. 'I'm perfectly capable of making my own arrangements,'

'You wish me to ring back and cancel?' Daniel suggested pleasantly.

She wanted to say yes, but she knew it would be foolish, especially when he'd obviously pulled strings to get the job done quickly. And sleeping out here in the living room for any longer than was absolutely necessary had no appeal at all.

'No,' she said reluctantly. 'Let's leave things as they are.'

'A wise choice,' he approved. 'You're learning.' He paused.

'I have to go into the office for a couple of hours, so you'll be able to pound your brother's ears with your objections over my unwanted presence to your little heart's content. Not,' he added, 'that it will make a blind bit of difference. The deal is done. But you might find it cathartic.'

He read the message conveyed by her over-bright eyes and compressed lips, and grinned.

'And keep off that ankle,' he advised. 'You need it to heal quickly. So that you can start pounding the pavements instead.'

Knowing that he spoke nothing but the truth did nothing to improve her temper or calm the riptide of emotion threatening to overwhelm her as she watched him walk away and go into her bedroom—*her bedroom*—closing the door behind him.

A shudder ran through her. What a mess, she thought. What a blinding, unbelievable mess. And how in God's name am I ever going to cope with it?

CHAPTER TWO

THE pain in her ankle was gradually turning to a dull throb. But the pain building inside her was a different matter. There was no quick fix for that, and it threatened to become unendurable more quickly than she could have imagined in her worst nightmares,

Yet she should have known, after these last two years of utter wretchedness. Months when she'd tried so hard to bury the hurt and bewilderment in the deepest recesses of her mind. And forget him.

Attempts that had never worked. That had eventually convinced her that only a complete change in her circumstances would do.

Which was why she'd made the reckless decision to relocate to Florida, without fully considering all the implications. Because she'd seen Andy's proposition as a chance for rehabilitation—a way of turning her life around and making a new start.

With an ocean—a whole continent—between Daniel and herself, she'd reasoned wildly, she might just stand a chance...

But now, after only just over a month, she was back, and in a worse situation than before. And shock and anger were fast giving way to total desperation as she contemplated what the weeks ahead of her would hold.

Seeing Daniel each day, she realised, her throat tightening. Knowing that he was sleeping only a matter of yards away every night. Oh, dear God...

She had a sudden image of him as he'd been that night, two

years ago, his tanned skin dark against the white towelling bathrobe, his face stark with disbelief in the moonlight as she'd told him, over and over again, her voice small and raw, the words stumbling against each other, that their marriage only a few hours earlier had been a terrible—a disastrous mistake. And that it was finished—over and done with—even before it had begun.

Forcing him to accept that she meant every word, and that there would be no second chance. Until at last he'd believed her, and turned away in bitter condemnation.

But he'd done as she wished. The marriage had been dissolved, more quickly and quietly than she'd believed possible.

What a strange word 'dissolved' was to use in the context of ending a marriage, she thought. It sounded almost gentle, implying that the relationship had been made to vanish, like rain falling on the earth. Not the agonised tearing apart—the destruction of her hopes and dreams—that had really taken place.

Nor had it led to Daniel simply disappearing from her life, as she'd hoped. Because once Laine had started living and working in London he'd been only too much in evidence.

She'd glimpsed him in the distance across crowded rooms. Looked down from the circle of a theatre to see him in the stalls, or discovered his picture in some paper or magazine. Never alone, either. The parade of his women seemed unending. Although, as she'd reminded herself wretchedly, that was only to be expected.

After all, he was a free man, in a way that she would never be a free woman. Because his heart had not been broken, or his life shattered, as hers had been.

But she'd never, mercifully, been close enough to him for their eyes to meet, or any greeting to be exchanged. Some atavistic instinct had always seemed to give her advance warning when he was around, enabling her to steel herself and move unobtrusively out of his orbit.

Until, of course, today, when her antennae had been disjointed—thrown into confusion by the events of the last forty-eight hours.

But how could I have thought—how could I possibly have dreamed—that something like this could happen? she asked herself, her throat tightening. Never—never in this world…

She checked, her heart thudding erratically against her ribs, as his door opened again. This time he was transformed into business formality, in elegant charcoal pants and an immaculate white shirt worn with a crimson silk tie. He was slotting thin gold links into his cuffs as he strode past her towards Jamie's bedroom without even glancing in her direction.

She found a voice. 'What are you doing?'

He said crisply, 'Making it possible for you to get to your bathroom without damaging that ankle even more.'

'Please don't bother.' Laine lifted her chin. 'I can cope perfectly well alone.'

He threw her a sardonic glance. 'Oh, that it were true.'

He pushed the door ajar and edged round it, and the next few minutes were filled with various brisk bangs and thuds, and a few muttered curses, while Laine sat chewing her lip.

She hated being forced to be beholden to him, even in the least respect, she thought furiously. But this would be the last time. She'd see to that.

From now on she would build a firewall round herself, she promised silently. Practise every avoidance tactic available. Because this was a question of sheer survival.

When Daniel came back, dusting off his hands, she was sitting rigidly upright, her face inimical.

'Thank you.' Her tone was ice.

'Gratitude,' he said, 'may not be your predominating emotion when you see the state of the bathroom.' He shrugged into his jacket and picked up his briefcase. 'But—that's your problem. One of many, I suspect.'

He paused, took a business card from his wallet, and tossed it down beside her. 'Jamie's contact number,' he said. 'I'm sure you'll want a word with him.' His smile grazed her. 'You both have some explaining to do.'

At the door, he took a final look back at her. 'And, talking of explanations, one of these days or nights—if the conversation palls—you might care to tell me why you put us both through that farce two years ago. Standing beside me in church, making vows you had no intention of keeping, even for twenty-four hours. When the simplest course would have been to call the whole thing off, saving us both a load of grief.' He allowed a heartbeat for her to assimilate that. Then, 'See you later,' he added with cool emphasis. And went.

'Look,' Jamie said with a defensiveness Laine could recognise even from the other side of the Atlantic, 'I didn't really have a choice. And what's the beef anyway? Okay, your marriage was a total fiasco, but that's long over, and I don't suppose he bears a grudge. Not after all this time.'

You think that? You really believe it?

'Anyway,' he added into the silence, 'there was a time when he was practically one of the family, especially after—after…'

'Don't,' Laine said, her voice suddenly husky. 'Just don't.' She took a deep breath, struggling with her composure. 'You have to understand that things are different now. And I—I don't think I can do this.'

'Oh, for heaven's sake.' His voice took on a peevish note. 'The two of us got by on a policy of strict non-interference, didn't we? Same roof, separate lives. And it will be the exactly same with Daniel.'

No, she said silently. It won't be. It can't… Because I've done that once before. And how can I live through that same nightmare all over again and remain sane?

'He's away a lot anyway,' he added. 'Visiting the corners of his far-flung empire. And when he is there, he certainly won't be sniffing round you, if that's what you're afraid of. Once bitten, twice shy.' He laughed. 'Besides, I've seen a sample of his current ladies, and you're not in the same league, sister dear.'

He had not, she thought, needed to tell her that. She knew it already. Had known it for too long.

She kept her voice steady. 'Thanks for the reassurance. Now, perhaps you'll tell me what he's doing here in our flat?'

He was silent for a moment. 'He bought a house a while back,' he said. 'He's been having it totally renovated—remodelled. Until it's finished he needs somewhere temporary to crash that doesn't involve long expensive leases with penalty clauses. It's that simple.'

'Forgive me,' Laine said grittily, 'if our ideas of simplicity don't quite coincide.' She paused. 'You haven't yet mentioned why you're working for him.'

'I needed a job. He made me an offer I couldn't refuse.'

'You had a job,' she said. 'At a decent firm. What happened?'

There was a silence, then he said, 'I got fired.'

'What?'

'Fired,' he repeated. 'As in sacked, let go, contract terminated.'

Laine felt as if she'd been punched in the stomach. 'What did you do?'

'Where shall I begin?' He paused theatrically. 'Inattention to detail. Poor time-keeping. Unexplained absences. Particularly those. They went through the procedures meticulously—written warnings, the lot. And I was found guilty on all charges.'

'This is—unbelievable.'

'Not really. Who wants to trust his business accounting to a guy who's hung over before noon? Old Balfour went through my client records like a ferret. I think he hoped they could make it a police matter.'

'Was that—possible?'

'No.' He paused. 'I may be a total idiot, Laine, but I don't have a death wish.'

'No?' she asked bitterly. 'Well, you could have fooled me. And this sudden departure to the States sounds very much like a moonlight flit. Please tell me I'm wrong.'

'You're like a bloody Rottweiler,' he said pettishly. 'You won't let go.'

'My God, do you blame me?' She drew a deep breath.

'Jamie—the truth. What kind of obligation are you under to Daniel Flynn?'

There was a silence, then he said grudgingly, 'I owe him—big time.'

It was the admission she'd least wanted to hear.

She said carefully, 'Do you mean that literally, or figuratively?'

'I mean it every which way,' he told her heavily. 'Six months ago I saved a client a lot of tax. He was grateful, and took me out to dinner. Afterwards we went to this gambling club, the Jupiter, where he was a member. We played roulette, and I won—quite a lot. Clive said I was a born gambler, and he sponsored me for membership. I started going back there. Once a week at first, and then more often. I won a little, but my losses soon began to mount up.

'That's when I ran into Daniel again. He was at the baccarat table one night. I could tell he was surprised to see me because the Jupiter catered for seriously high rollers. He invited me to have a drink with him, a chat about old times. But I soon realised he was trying to warn me off—advise me not to get in too deep. He said the Jupiter had something of a reputation. But I wasn't prepared to listen.'

He continued impatiently, 'I won't make excuses, Laine. It was too late. I was already over my head, heavily in debt and unable to pay, and the club wanted its money.

'I'd got to know Sandra, one of the croupiers, and she warned me that there were—people looking for me. That's when I went to ground. Stayed away from the flat. Didn't go to work. I—I've never been so scared in my life.

'Eventually Daniel found me,' he continued heavily. 'I was—staying with Sandra's cousin, and he persuaded her to give him the address. Said there was a family connection, and he wanted to help.'

'Family connection?' Laine echoed with angry derision. 'My God, he has a damned nerve.'

'Well, he was momentarily my brother-in-law. And what would you have preferred?' He was angry too. 'For me to be found in some alley, beaten to a pulp? In hospital with two broken legs? Daniel was a total bastard—he played absolute hell with me—but he also saved my life. Not for my sake. He made it damned clear that he thinks I'm pretty much a waste of good space.' There was a faint choke in his voice. 'No, he helped me only because he knows that Simon would have done the same.'

She said numbly, 'Yes—of course, he would…'

'So,' Jamie went on, 'he paid off the club, and got Sandra out of it, too, in case her bosses found out she'd been helping me and—objected.

'That's why he offered me a job in New York. He said we might find the climate healthier than London for the next few months. I told you—I don't have a death wish, so I agreed. Letting him use the flat seemed a pretty small return, all things considered.' There was a pause. 'And, to be fair, I didn't think you'd ever find out.'

'Except I have, and now I'm being punished for your misdemeanours,' Laine said with renewed crispness.

'Well, that won't worry him,' Jamie said with a touch of weariness. 'To be honest, he doesn't seem to have a lot of time for either of us.'

He paused, 'Anyway, what exactly are you doing back in the UK? Is the business doing so well that you can afford a holiday?'

No point in pretence. 'There is no business. Not any more.'

'You have to be kidding.' His tone was incredulous. 'Everyone wants to go fishing off the Florida Keys. It's a licence to print money.'

'Perhaps,' she said. 'But Andy decided to sell the licence.'

'At a healthy profit, I hope?'

'I imagine so,' Laine said, her voice bright and brittle. 'Unfortunately he never discussed it with me—before, during or after the transaction. Particularly after. I got back from trying to find us some alternative office premises and found it was a done deal and that Andy had—moved on.' She took a breath. 'I—decided against looking for him.'

He said slowly, 'You mean—he took—everything? But you invested in that boat—every penny you had.'

'So I did,' she said. 'But unfortunately I ended up with a nil return, silly me.'

There was a silence, then he said, 'My God, Laine, I'm sorry.'

'Don't be,' she said, crisply. 'I reckon in many ways I got off quite cheaply.'

'Perhaps,' he said. 'But I genuinely thought you were happy—settled. That you were making yourself a life.'

'I suppose I did too.' *But is that really the truth, or was I simply buying myself some time while I waited for the healing process to work?*

'However,' she went on, 'it's left me in a bit of a spot, financially. And I rather hoped you'd be around—to help.'

'Well, I would be,' he said. 'Under normal circumstances. But my salary level at Wordwide isn't brilliant, and I have to start repaying Daniel.'

He paused awkwardly. 'And there's Sandra. She's got a job in a diner. The money's putrid, so she has to rely on tips to boost it. We're having quite a struggle.' Another pause. 'What about the gallery? Couldn't you get your old job back?'

'Unlikely. They'll have replaced me long ago.'

'I suppose so.' A longer silence. 'You could always try Ma.'

'No,' she said, quietly. 'That's one of several things I won't even consider.'

'Daniel being another?'

'The prime example,' she confirmed. 'Besides, it's clear that you've used up any residue of goodwill he may have had towards the Sinclair family.'

'You could try being nice to him,' Jamie suggested.

Her voice was suddenly husky. 'What the hell do you mean?'

'Well, not what you're thinking, obviously.' He was defensive again. 'But when you were a kid you used to follow him round like a puppy. And there must have been a time when he liked you too, or he wouldn't have asked you to marry him. And even

though it turned into a disaster, you might catch him at a senti-
mental moment.'

'I don't think he has them.' Laine found herself sinking her
teeth into her lower lip. 'No, from here on I'm strictly on my own,
but I'll manage. Watch me.'

'Is Daniel around now?'

'He went to his office.' She added coldly, 'He looked the
image of a man about to make his next million.'

'Well, don't knock it,' Jamie said, with something of a snap.
'I've no idea what happened between you two years ago, and I
don't want to know. However, I'll just say this.' His voice
became urgent. 'For God's sake take it easy where he's concerned, and don't go out of your way to upset him, Laine,
whatever you may feel. Because I can't afford it. And maybe you
can't either.'

He paused. 'Keep in touch.'

Laine replaced the receiver, and sat for a long while, staring
into space.

Any fleeting plan of having the locks changed in Daniel's
absence no longer seemed to be an option, she thought, her
mouth twisting.

She realised she wasn't shocked or even particularly surprised
by Jamie's tale of woe. He seemed to have been tottering from
one disaster to the next since adolescence. Flirtations with
alcohol and drugs had led to expulsion from two schools, and
he'd distinguished himself at the third with a brief and unsuc-
cessful career as a bookmaker in the sixth form. Only the fact
that his final public examinations were looming had saved him
from yet another ignominious exit.

His time at university, however, had been relatively peaceful,
and he'd apparently transferred seamlessly to Cowper Dymond.

Laine had hoped her brother's problems were behind him, but
how wrong could anyone be?

She supposed he was not entirely to blame. As their family
life had begun to fall apart it was Jamie who'd absorbed most of

the resultant pressure. Their mother's dependency had been transferred to him.

Nobody expected very much of me, Laine thought. I was the youngest. The baby. The little sister.

She replaced the phone on its rest, and stood up. The ice pack had helped reduce some of the swelling to her ankle, and she'd apply another one later.

But now she had things to do. And making Jamie's room at least habitable was the first of them. Comfort could follow once the place had been emptied tomorrow.

As Daniel had piled everything neatly in one corner, she could actually move around it as long as she was careful. She began by clearing her clothes from the bed, and hanging them in the fitted wardrobes, alongside the few things Jamie had left, then filling the empty drawers in his dressing chest.

She fetched clean linen and made up the bed, before devoting half an hour's energetic cleaning to the scruffy bathroom, throwing away half-used toiletries and oddments of soap, and scouring the basin and tub.

Particularly the tub—because she had plans for that.

When basic hygiene had been restored, she stripped and put on her favourite robe, an elderly blue velour, much rubbed, but as comforting as a hug from a friend.

She unpacked her bag and put the modest amount of clothing it contained into the washing machine, along with the garments she'd just discarded. Her precipitate departure meant that she'd had to leave much of her stuff behind.

I seem to be spending my entire life in flight, one way or another, she derided herself. But now the thing I've dreaded most has happened, so there's no point in running any more.

Finally, she ran herself a generous bath, scenting it lavishly with her favourite oil. She gave her hair a vigorous shampoo using the hand-shower, before sinking down with a grateful sigh into the water, immersing herself to the tops of her breasts. She leaned back, closing her eyes as the fragrant warmth caressed her skin.

This was heaven. The shower on the boat had been intermittent at best, and at times totally non-cooperative. Her last exchange with Andy had been on that very subject. She'd said they must get it fixed before the next season. He'd grunted.

Nothing new in that, she thought. But maybe she should have reckoned up the number of grunts per conversation and drawn some kind of conclusion from them. Then she might have been more prepared for his selling their only asset and doing a runner with the proceeds.

She'd known, of course, that Andy bitterly resented the fact that she'd refused any physical involvement with him, and supposed he could not, in truth, be blamed for that. However, she'd made no actual promises, she told herself defensively.

It had been the chance of a new life halfway across the world, out of harm's way, that she'd wanted. Not him. And she'd agreed to go with him just as his business partner, not his lover. He should have taken nothing for granted.

But he was a good-looking example of the blond, curly haired, rugged corner of the market, and charming with it—on the surface at least—so he probably hadn't had too many rejections in his life. No doubt he'd believed that proximity would do its work, and that he'd persuade her round to his way of thinking in due course.

Well, she thought with a swift shiver, at least I was spared that. The money was all he got from me.

He'd totally underestimated her indifference to him sexually, just as she'd completely missed the signs that beneath the charismatic son-of-the-sea pose was a common swindler.

A brilliant fisherman, of course, in every way. Bait the hook, she thought bitterly, and reel 'em in.

But they'd had a good business going there, she reflected with regret. Their clientele had registered few complaints, and an abundance of compliments, especially about the good food she'd managed to produce in a galley that just bordered on the adequate, and money had been there to be made. But she could see now that, outside the thrill and glamour of the chase for the big game fish, it had all been too much like hard work for Andy. He wanted easy pickings, and no slog over bookkeeping or maintenance.

In retrospect, she could see she should have been warned that all might not be as it seemed. Except that she hadn't allowed herself time to think—or to wonder what she might be getting into.

Oh, his proposition that she should invest in his business had come at exactly the right moment, she thought, her mouth twisting in self-derision. And when you're thrown a lifeline, you don't always check the rope for durability. You're just too thankful to be rescued...

Dear God—some rescue! As she'd come back to the boat that day, weary and disheartened by lack of success in finding their business the new shore premises it needed, she had already known that persuading Andy to sit down and talk through their current difficulties would present a mammoth problem.

So, she'd not anticipated an easy time. She had, however, expected that he'd be there. Not that she'd find the revolting Dirk Clemmens waiting for her down in the saloon, a bottle of bourbon open on the table in front of him beside a sheaf of papers.

Of all their clients, this wealthy South African had been her least favourite. She'd loathed the way he made any excuse to touch her, brushing past her unnecessarily close. Making sure their hands met when she passed him a drink or served food. She didn't like the friends he brought with him either, overweight and loud-mouthed. Or the girls who lay around sun-bathing, wearing only thongs when not completely naked.

Andy's mouth had curled, however, when she'd complained about Clemmens and his groping. 'Why should you care?' he'd demanded sullenly. 'We both know he's on a hiding to nothing with you, sweetheart.'

And, suddenly, inexplicably, the burly South African had been right there, back on the boat, and she'd seemed to be alone with him, which had bewildered her as well as filling her with an odd sense of foreboding. But she'd hidden it well, keeping her voice cool. 'Where's Andy?'

'Oh, he's gone.' He sounded almost casual. 'We did a deal, chickie, and I'm now the new owner—in full possession.' He had soft pink lips that always looked wet, and he stretched them now in an ingratiating smile. 'Welcome back.'

Laine had stayed very still. She said quietly, 'There must be some mistake. Andy and I were partners.'

'Yeah, he told me. Sleeping partners.' He gave a lascivious chuckle. 'Which suits me just fine—so let's keep the arrangement going, shall we?' He pushed a glass towards her. 'Sit down, honey. Have a drink while we discuss your—duties, eh?'

She said desperately, 'But surely he must have left me a message of some kind?'

'Yeah, he did. Now, how did he put it?' He pretended to think for a moment. 'Oh, I remember. He said to tell you, "So long, honey, and don't think it wasn't nice."'

The shock of what he was saying brought bile into her throat, but it seemed wiser to take a seat while she tried to assimilate the full horror of Andy's defection, and this resultant change in her circumstances.

She poured some whisky into her glass, and took a minimal sip as she waited for her mind to stop reeling.

Andy, she thought. *Andy*—whom she'd trusted—had done this to her. Had cheated her, stolen from her, and left her to this *creature*, whom he knew she hated. Was this his idea of revenge for turning him down—to abandon her to the mercies of a man whom she knew wouldn't take no for an answer?

Was every man she came across going to betray her in some way?

Her stomach churned as she tried to think what to do next. Her instinct was screaming to her to make a dash for it, but, although Clemmens was a big man, he was light on his feet, and she wasn't sure she could out-run him. And the thought of being caught by him—subdued—was terrifying.

No she would have to be more clever than that. Besides, she couldn't simply leave empty-handed. Her wallet, with what ready money she possessed, was with her in her shoulder bag, but her passport was in her cabin with the rest of her things, and she needed it.

However, he'd clearly been celebrating his purchase, and this could work in her favour. She'd seen him drink before and, despite appearances and his own bragging, he didn't have the hardest head in Miami.

She waited until he started shuffling through the papers, muttering with satisfaction, then swiftly tipped her drink down her skirt. It felt horribly clammy, and she immediately stank of spirits, but she could only hope Clemmens had imbibed enough himself not to notice that.

She poured another modest amount for herself, then refilled his glass, pushing it within easy reach. His fingers closed round it, and he drank.

He wiped his mouth with his fist, belched, and looked at her. 'Andy tells me that once you're in the sack you're not nearly as prim and proper as you make out, sweetie.' He laughed again. 'I sure hope that's true, because I pay by results.'

She smiled at him. Raised her glass in a semi-toast. 'Then I trust you're prepared to be generous, Mr Clemmens.'

Andy, you total bastard! Whatever you've done with the money, you could have spared me this—animal.

She sipped, then sent the rest over her skirt, as he splashed more bourbon into his glass, spattering his papers in the process.

He swore. 'Get a cloth.'

She obeyed reluctantly, hoping he wouldn't notice her damp skirt. But he simply grabbed the cloth from her hand, and began to dab clumsily at the top document.

'God, it's hot in here.' He ran a finger round the collar of his polo shirt. 'Isn't there a fan or something?'

'There used to be.' She shrugged. 'Maybe Andy took it with him.'

'No, he took nothing but the asking price. I saw to that.'

Her heart skipped a beat, but her tone held nothing but indifference. 'Then it'll be somewhere in the guest quarters.'

'Well, don't just sit there.' He leaned back against the cushioned seat, closing his eyes. 'Get it.'

Laine rose and picked up her bag from the side of her chair. Was it really going to be this easy?

She went straight to the tiny space she'd occupied since she came on board, and changed swiftly out of her ruined skirt into a pair of white jeans.

She retrieved her passport, and thrust as much as she could carry into the smaller of her two travel bags, knowing that she needed to travel light.

Then, soft-footed, she went up on deck. She'd just stepped on to the gangplank when Dirk Clemmens' voice sounded just behind her. 'Where d'you think you're going, chickie? You come here, now, like a good girl.'

As he reached for her Laine ran, hurling herself headlong on to the dock. Clemmens, panting close behind, made a grab for her but missed, and, bawling with rage, overbalanced and fell flat.

Laine, landing awkwardly, twisted her ankle, but kept going somehow, biting her lip against the pain. A glance over her shoulder showed that a small crowd was already gathering round Clemmens, who was trying to sit up.

She heard his voice like a wounded bull. 'Stop her—she's a thief.' But she didn't falter, or slacken her pace. She received a few curious looks, but no one attempted to detain her.

She turned abruptly and dodged into a bar that she knew, and made her way through the groups of drinkers as if on her way to the women's room. Once at the rear, she took the emergency exit instead, finding herself in a quiet backstreet.

However, she'd shot her bolt, and she knew it. She was limping heavily now, and her ankle was swelling up like a balloon, so she hailed the first cruising cab she saw and asked to be taken to the airport.

And now here I am, she thought mirthlessly, as she climbed

out of the bath and swathed herself in a towel. Out of the frying pan, straight into the inferno.

She towelled herself down swiftly, then rubbed the excess moisture from her hair and combed it back from her face with her fingers, grimacing as she remembered that her hairdryer was one of the items she'd been forced to abandon on the boat.

But I had a spare one here, she thought, getting back into her robe. I kept it in my dressing table.

Will it still be there—and do I have the nerve to check?

Yet, it was safe enough, she assured herself. Daniel was at the office, and she was surely entitled to retrieve her own property?

She limped across the living area, pushed open the door of her bedroom, and went cautiously inside—only to pause with a small, shocked gasp as she looked around her.

Because it was unrecognisable. The pretty wallpaper with its delicate tracery of honeysuckle had been painted over in plain ivory, and her pale yellow silk bedcover had been replaced by something far more austere in dark brown. The curtains were brown too, and even the bedside rugs had been changed.

Every trace of her, every charming personal touch that her earnings from the gallery had provided, seemed to have been deliberately erased.

They say you shouldn't go back, she thought, because you'll find the space you occupied has gone.

And I'm suddenly beginning to feel as if I no longer exist.

As if everything I loved most has been taken away from me. My father first, when I was a baby, then Simon, and eventually Abbotsbrook. Maybe it was never the sanctuary I imagined, and my last memories of it were pretty hideous, but it held a kind of security all the same.

I always thought one day I'd go back, and somehow rediscover everything that was precious from my childhood.

She bit her lip. Oh, come on, now, she adjured herself impatiently. You're here to dry your hair, not collapse into sentimentality.

She took a breath, then raised her head and looked across the room into the dressing table mirror. If Daniel hadn't changed, there was little difference in her either. Her hair was still mousy, albeit streaked by the sun, and her figure remained like a stick. Her eyes would always be more grey than green, although she did have her mother's cheekbones, which perhaps redeemed her face from being totally nondescript.

But not a great deal to set, all the same, against Daniel's known preferences in womankind. The glamorous leggy blondes with the knowing eyes who'd made her adolescence miserable.

Or Candida, she thought, flinching as she recalled the sultry mouth, the body that swayed inside its clothes as if impatient to be free of them, and the sweet husky voice like poisoned honey.

How could any man resist her?

Deep within her something twisted in renewed agony, and she heard herself gasp.

'Do not,' she said aloud, her voice vehement. 'Do not go there.'

But it was too late. And suddenly it was all too much, the throb in her ankle swamped by this other fiercer pain. She was alone, broke and scared. And she'd been through forty-eight hours of sheer trauma only to find a different kind of hell waiting for her in the place that should have been her refuge.

And Laine put her hands over her face, sank down on the edge of that immaculately smooth, alien bed, and wept, her whole body shaking with her sobs, until she had no more tears left.

CHAPTER THREE

FOR a long time after she was calm again Laine remained where she was, lying face downward on the bed, her fingers digging almost convulsively into the quilted satin of the bedcover.

But she knew she couldn't stay there. Recognised, in fact, it would have been better if she'd never entered the room at all. Because Daniel was here, all around her, tormenting her senses and her memory.

The faint scent of his cologne was in the air. The subtle musky fragrance she'd always associated with him. That she'd breathed in so many times in the past with all the helpless longing of first love.

'Time I wasn't here,' she said aloud.

She got slowly to her feet, meticulously restoring the coverlet to its former pristine condition. Making sure there was no untoward sign of her presence. And she managed to find her hairdryer, too—not where she'd left it, of course, but at the back of a shelf in the row of immaculately organised wardrobes.

Out of sight—out of mind, she thought as she crossed the living area to the other room. Rather like myself.

He'll probably never know it's gone.

And at that same moment she heard the rattle of a key in the front door.

Oh, God, she thought, her heart thudding. He's back. I got out just in time.

She tossed the hairdryer onto the bed, and turned defensively, pulling the door shut behind her as Daniel came in. He looked preoccupied and not particularly good-tempered.

'Oh, it's you,' she said stiltedly, wincing at the absurdity of the remark.

His tone was acid. 'Who were you expecting?'

'Well, not you. Not so soon.' She paused. 'You—startled me.'

'I can see that,' he said brusquely. 'You look like a ghost.' He walked over to her, putting a finger under her chin as his frowning gaze scanned her face.

'Don't.' Laine pushed his hand away.

'You've been crying,' he said. 'Why?'

'Is it any concern of yours?'

'Probably not. But I've no wish to share my living space with the human equivalent of a leaking tap.' His mouth tightened. 'Do us both a favour, Laine, and give some thought to growing up.'

He walked over to the other room, disappearing briefly to emerge a moment later with a laptop computer in a carrying case slung over his shoulder.

She braced herself, but he made no comment, so it seemed she'd covered her tracks successfully.

'See you later,' he tossed at her as he passed.

'As if I had a choice,' she returned bitterly as the door closed behind him.

And he would, of course, catch her looking like something the cat dragged in, with wet hair and her old robe. Although that was probably safer, under the circumstances. The last thing she wanted was for him to feel even a momentary attraction to her. Not that it was likely, she reminded herself, and went into her room to dry her hair.

Although thick, it was soft and fine, and needed skilful layering to give it any real shape. No chance of that, however, until she discovered just how dire her financial situation was, she thought as she put down her brush.

She dressed swiftly in a blue denim skirt and a thin, collarless white blouse. Her ankle was still making her flinch whenever she put weight on it, so she fetched some more ice cubes and stretched out on the sofa, resting the aching joint on a cushion.

But she couldn't completely relax. Her mind was buzzing—on fire—teeming with stray images from the past, all as vivid as they were unwelcome.

Reminding her starkly that she could barely remember a time when she hadn't been in love with him.

Recalling the day when, at six years old, she'd emerged on hands and knees from her special den in the garden and looked up to see him—this stranger—standing at Simon's side, tall and dark against the sunlight.

'I told you this is where she'd be,' her brother had said, his voice teasing and affectionate. 'Jamie built this little place as a hide, so he could watch birds, but as usual he got bored with it, and now it's Laine's. Get up, scrap, and be polite to my mate Daniel.'

As she scrambled to her feet, she said with dignity, 'It's my *secret* place. You're not meant to tell.'

Daniel bent and carefully removed a dead leaf from her hair. 'My lips are sealed,' he said. 'I promise.' He paused. 'Are you a birdwatcher too?'

She shook her head. 'I come here to read.'

'What's the book of the moment?'

She looked back longingly. '*Treasure Island.*'

'Good God,' he said, exchanging amused glances with Simon. 'So, who's your favourite character?'

She gave it some thought. 'I don't think any of them are very nice. They're all greedy, and Jim spies on people.' She paused. 'Ben Gunn isn't too bad, I suppose, because he only wants toasted cheese.'

'You heard it here first, folks,' Simon said, grinning. 'Stevenson, eat your heart out. Come on, Dan, let's leave her to her pirates and get some tennis in before tea.' He ruffled her hair, dislodging more dead leaves. 'See you later, Lainie. And clean up a bit before Ma sees you. She seems a bit agitated today.'

'That's because Mr Latimer was here yesterday,' Laine informed him. 'She's always in a bad mood after that, because she hates him. She calls him that "bloody man".'

There was a brief silence, then Dan turned away, apparently overcome by a coughing fit, while Simon looked down at his younger sibling, his young face suddenly weary.

He said quietly, 'But you don't have to do the same, Lainie. Is that understood?'

She said uncertainly 'Are you cross too?'

'No,' he said, forcing a smile. 'No, of course not. It's just that a visit from the trustee isn't the ideal start to a vacation.'

It was good that Simon was home, Laine thought contentedly, as they departed and she went back to her book. Because it meant that Mummy would stop frowning, and smile instead.

The housekeeper, Mrs Evershott always sounded the gong for meals five minutes early, so she gauged she'd have plenty of time to wash her hands and comb her hair before tea.

But that day her mother had arranged for it to be served on the lawn, as a tribute to the good weather, and there was no way she could reach the house unobserved.

'Elaine!' Angela exclaimed from the shelter of her parasol. 'What have you been doing? Rolling in mud? And where's your hair ribbon?' She turned to the others at the table, shrugging helplessly. 'What a ragamuffin. A cupboard full of pretty dresses, and she insists on those old shorts.'

She sighed. 'I don't think her poor father would recognise his Lily Maid these days.'

'Lily Maid?' Daniel queried politely, while Laine stared down at the grass, shuffling her feet in their blue flip-flops, knowing what was coming next, and dreading it.

Angela sighed again. 'My mother-in-law was a big Tennyson fan, and when she saw the baby for the first time she was folded in a white shawl—looking like a lily, apparently. So Mama persuaded Graham to christen her Elaine, after the girl in the poem—*The Lily Maid of Astolat*.'

There was a pause, then Dan said politely, 'That's a charming story.'

'No, it isn't,' Laine said with sudden fierceness. 'Elaine's a silly name, and Jamie says she was a wuss for dying just because Sir Lancelot wasn't in love with her—and he says I'll grow up to be a wuss, too, because I'm called after her.'

There was an odd silence, then Simon put down his plate and began to laugh, to be joined by Dan and eventually Angela.

'It's a bad day for literature in this house,' Simon managed at last, wiping his eyes. 'And we're laughing *with* you, scruff, not at you. Now, come and have some tea, and I'll have a word with Master Jamie when he shows up.'

Everyone had laughed that summer, Laine thought. It was one of the happiest she'd ever spent, and the start of many more.

And she'd had Simon and Daniel to thank for that.

Up to then, she'd been left pretty much to her own devices in the school holidays. Unlike Jamie, who'd attended a local preparatory school as a day boy prior to following Simon to their father's old school in the autumn, Laine had made few friends locally. The other children at the village school, finding that she wasn't interested in the latest junior fashions, and that she preferred reading to the television programmes they all seemed to watch, had tended to ignore her.

And even with her beloved books she'd found herself lonely at times.

But that holiday had been altogether different. The weather had been good, so they'd all been able to spend as much time outside as possible. And Laine had been included in all their activities. It had all been casual—no big deal. She'd just been expected to accompany them.

Until then she'd always been faintly nervous of the river that bordered the end of the Abbotsbrook grounds. She'd been learning to swim at school, but Angela had said firmly that the river was a very different proposition from the swimming baths in the nearby market town, and that Laine must keep well away from it at all times.

But Simon and Daniel had changed all that. Under their eagle-eyed supervision, her technique and confidence had surged ahead, until, as Simon had told their mother, she could swim like a fish.

'Or an eel,' Jamie had put in. 'Eel-Laine.' And he'd continued to torment her with the nickname, roaring with laughter at his own wit, until Daniel had taken him quietly to one side and stopped it.

But none of Jamie's teasing had had the power to upset her. She'd been far too happy.

Some of the best days had been spent out on the water in the old dinghy. When the boys had fished, she'd been provided with a small rod and line to hunt for tiddlers.

If they'd played cricket she had cheerfully fielded for them, and had zealously located balls that had been hit into the shrubbery from the tennis court.

Most of all, they'd both talked to her as if they were genuinely interested in what she had to say.

But the holiday had ended far too soon for Laine. Simon had joined his school's climbing club the year before, and had become swiftly and seriously addicted to the sport, so he'd been taking the last two weeks of his vacation in the Lake District, while Daniel had been summoned to join his father for a rare break in the South of France.

As goodbyes had been said, Laine had launched herself at Daniel, arms and legs wrapped round him, clinging like a monkey. Hugging him strenuously, she'd whispered, 'I wish you were my brother, too.'

'Elaine!' Angela reproved. 'Kindly stop making a spectacle of yourself. Daniel, do put the wretched child down. I must apologise to you for this ridiculous behaviour.'

'It's not a problem, Mrs Sinclair.' He lowered Laine gently to the ground, ruffling her hair. 'Please believe I'm very flattered.'

'Also very tolerant.' She offered him a limpid smile. 'But you're not a babysitter, you know. Perhaps on your visit at Christmas we can all do some rather more grown-up things.'

There was a brief, odd silence, then he said quietly, 'Of course.'

Christmas, Laine thought ecstatically. He would be back at Christmas. He and Simon. And that would be the best present she could have.

Hero-worship, she told herself wearily, as she got up from the sofa to take the bag of melting ice cubes back to the kitchen. That was what it had been. The world's most gigantic crush. A childish phase that she should have outgrown quite easily.

However, for the next five years, her entire life had seemed to take its focus from school and university vacations, and she'd waited for them with almost painful eagerness, knowing that Daniel would join them for a week or two at least.

Not that the holidays had been unalloyed delight any more. As she'd got older Laine had become aware that were undercurrents beneath Abbotsbrook's seemingly tranquil surface. And that Mr Latimer's all too regular visits were invariably a cause of friction.

She'd been curled up on the window-seat in her room one spring evening, when her mother's voice, raised in complaint, had reached her from the terrace below.

'I thought everything would change when you were eighteen,' Angela was saying. 'That you could persuade the wretched little man to keep his distance.'

He said tiredly, 'Ma, the trust will stay in force until Jamie and Laine are both eighteen. You have to accept that.' He paused. 'And you'd see less of Latimer if you curbed your spending a little. Fewer weekend parties, maybe?'

'Your father started them. And it's the only way I can keep in touch with our friends when I'm buried down here all year round. I wish to heaven I could sell the place and move back to London.'

'You know the terms of Dad's will,' he said. 'I'm afraid you'll have to wait until Laine comes of age for that—if you still want to.'

'I'll want to,' she said. 'If the house is still standing, that is. The damned place is falling apart, and Latimer won't release enough money to do what's necessary. Then I have to put up with people treating the place as a shrine—turning up in droves so they can see the room—the desk—where he created "all those amazing fantasy novels, Mrs Sinclair",' she added, in a savage mimicry of a Transatlantic accent.

'And I'm sick of them telling me what a tragedy it was he was taken so soon. Do they think I don't know that? I'm his widow, for God's sake. And he wasn't "taken". It was a heart attack, not abduction by aliens.'

'Well, don't knock the faithful fans,' Simon advised crisply. 'After all, it's Dad's royalties that have been paying the bills, and frankly they're not as good as they were a few years ago. In fact, I wonder...'

They moved away, and Laine heard no more. She sat, arms clasping her knees, feeling suddenly very cold. Surely nothing could happen to Abbotsbrook? *Surely?* It might be big and old, and need repairs, but it was their home.

The subject of money was raised again the following night after supper, this time by Simon, as he settled down to a game of chess with Dan.

He said casually, 'I suppose Lainie will be finishing at the village school at the end of the summer. Have you decided where she'll be going next? Sent for some prospectuses?'

Angela poured herself some more coffee. 'No, I haven't. Her recent reports haven't been exactly thrilling, so I thought she might as well go to Hollingbury Comprehensive with the rest of her class. As I still have Jamie's fees to cope with, it seems an ideal way to economise a little.'

Simon sat up abruptly. 'Ma, you can't be serious. Hollingbury Comp is a dump. Everyone knows that it barely scraped through its Ofsted inspection, and it has a drugs problem. Lainie wouldn't have a prayer.'

'I gather the staff are working very hard to improve things,' Angela said repressively. 'Besides, Laine's hardly a high-flier, you know. If she'd tried a little harder, things might be different.'

Laine felt heat invade her face, and her mouth trembled as everyone looked at her.

After a pause, Daniel said quietly, 'I realise I have no right to interfere in a family matter, Mrs Sinclair, but I've always considered Laine a very bright girl. I wonder if she could simply be bored at her present school, and in need of more of a challenge.'

His smile held apology as well as charm. 'My godfather's daughters both went to a place called Randalls, which has an excellent reputation.' He added levelly, 'And it offers full bursaries to pupils with genuine potential. I think Laine could be one of them, so fees wouldn't be a problem.'

He paused. 'There's a written test as well as an interview, I believe, but I could easily get hold of some details—if that isn't too presumptuous?'

'Not at all.' Angela smiled at him. 'I'm just not sure that Laine's up to it.'

'Well, I think, along with Dan, that she should be given the benefit of the doubt,' Simon said firmly.

The next time Laine saw Daniel, at the beginning of the summer holidays, she danced across the hall to him in excitement. 'I did it—I did it. I'm going to Randalls in September.'

His brows lifted quizzically. 'So you survived the exam?'

She considered. 'Well, it wasn't a real one, with sums and things. I just had to write about a favourite character from a book.'

His face relaxed into a teasing grin. 'Now, let me guess. How about—Ben Gunn?'

She gasped. 'How did you know that?'

'I have a good memory,' he said. 'Besides, I knew it wouldn't be the Lily Maid. Why write about a wuss?' He paused. 'Is your mother pleased?'

'Yes,' she said a little doubtfully. Angela had been more astonished than pleased, she thought, and had drawn a sharp breath when the school uniform list arrived. 'Oh, yes.' She gave him an uncertain look. 'Are *you* pleased, too?'

'Over the moon.' He picked her up and swung her round. 'It's a good school, and you'll have a great time.'

From the doorway, a girl's voice said coolly, 'Is this a private party, or can anyone join in?'

Laine saw the newcomer over Daniel's shoulder—a tall, leggy blonde, in tiny shorts and a cut-off top that barely covered her breasts.

She looked, Laine thought with disfavour, like one of the Barbie dolls her former classmates had used to bring to school.

Daniel set Laine down without haste, and turned as the girl came wandering over, tossing back her hair, and allowing a condescending smile to play about her full lips as she studied the slight, childish figure standing in front of her.

'You're full of surprises, darling.' She slid an arm through Daniel's, pressing herself against him with possessive intimacy. 'I'd never have figured you as the paternal type. So, who's the baby?'

A protest rose to Laine's lips, but she swallowed it back, concealing it behind the poker-face she'd learned to assume when trouble loomed.

Daniel said evenly, 'She's Simon's little sister—as you probably knew already. So don't waste your ammunition, Candida, my sweet, because you may well need it later. Now, why don't you give Si a hand to get his stuff together for the vacation?'

'Because I'm not anyone's slave.' She kissed him lingeringly on the cheek. 'Even yours. And he sent me to say that, unless you help him repack the boot, there may not be room for it.'

His sideways glance was faintly caustic. 'On the other hand, you could unload some of your own cases. That would make more space.'

'Darling.' Her voice grew throaty. 'You'd hardly want me to walk round the villa naked for the next three weeks.' She giggled. 'Or would you?'

'My father's other guests might well object.' He detached himself gently. 'Now, behave yourself and wait in the drawing room while Laine tells her mother that we're here.'

Her task accomplished, Laine went upstairs and found Simon in his room, hurriedly stowing clothes in a travel bag.

'Come to help, scrap? Pass me those T-shirts, will you?'

She handed them to him. 'Aren't you going to be here for the holidays?'

He heard the wistful note in her voice, and his tone was kind. 'Not this time, honey. Daniel's father's bought a place in Tuscany, and we're driving down there for our last few weeks of freedom before we get trapped in the workplace.'

She was silent for a moment. 'Is that lady with Daniel?'

'Candy? Yes, she is. Why?'

'I don't think she's very nice.' Laine concentrated on refolding some swimming shorts.

His lips twitched. 'Now, that,' he said solemnly, 'might depend on your point of view. And I'm sure Dan has no complaints.'

There was a stone lodged in her chest. 'Is he going to marry her?'

He burst out laughing. 'Good God, no. Our Daniel is definitely not the marrying kind. I can't see him ever allowing a wife to cramp his style. And this holiday is all strictly casual.'

He studied her for a moment. 'One day you'll have boyfriends of your own, Lainie, and then you'll understand that not all relationships need to be serious.'

He walked over to her and hugged her. 'Congratulations on getting into Randalls, by the way. It's just what you need, and you'll do well there. Things are looking up for you, scrap.'

Were they? Laine wondered as she trailed along the landing. Then why did she feel that the sunlit day had suddenly become dull and full of clouds?

She decided not to go downstairs again, but sought her own bedroom instead, curling up on her favourite window seat and leaning her forehead listlessly against the glass panes.

She kept seeing the way that girl's hand had touched Daniel's arm, the pink-tipped fingers stroking his tanned skin. How her body had seemed to curve into his, as if they were part of each other.

There'd been sex education at her school, and she wasn't sure what she'd hated most—her form teacher's brisk resumé of the physical facts, or the sniggering crudities exchanged in the play-ground by her classmates.

Suddenly she felt unhappily that those few awkward moments in the hall had taught her far more about what happened between a man and a woman—and that it was a lesson she could have well done without.

And, although she did not realise it until much later, that reve-lation marked the end of her childhood.

Not the marrying kind… Nine years further on, Simon's pro-phetic words seemed to resound in her brain, and she shook her head impatiently, trying to block them out.

It was time she stopped tormenting herself like this, she thought. What point was there in going back to the past, when it was the present and the future that were going to cause her the real problems?

She stood, looking around the kitchen as if she'd never seen it before.

It was incredibly neat, and immaculately clean, with none of the cheerful clutter that a keen cook might accumulate. The only other change she noticed was the addition of a state-of-the-art coffee machine, which Daniel clearly must save for dinner party use, because she'd only rated a mug of instant.

Oh, get over yourself, she adjured herself impatiently, her mouth twisting. You're hungry. That's what's the matter with you, my girl. Your metabolism's low, and your spirits are down to match.

You can get through this—but not by turning a drama into a tragedy.

You need to play it cool from now on. Make it clear that now you've recovered from the initial surprise of seeing him you can deal with it in a civilised way. And that you are grown up.

Because none of it matters any more. It can't be allowed to matter, if you're to retain your grip on your sanity. And if you make too big a fuss you could give him the impression that you still care.

She shivered, her hands balling into fists at her side.

She said aloud, 'Nothing lasts for ever, and this—situation, too, will pass. It's just a temporary thing.'

And maybe Jamie's advice was sound, for once, and a small gesture of reconciliation was called for. So—she would prepare a meal for them both.

At the same time she wanted to prove to him, even in a small way, that she was not the lightweight he seemed to imagine, and that her time on the boat had not been a pleasure cruise, but hard graft.

If nothing else, at least she might gain a modicum of respect.

There was little enough in the freezer, but she retrieved a pack of chicken portions and defrosted them in the microwave. She found onions and garlic in the vegetable rack, and jars of capers and black olives, along with tinned tomatoes and dried pasta in the storage cupboard, and began her preparations.

This is what it might have been like, she thought suddenly, if we'd had a real marriage. I'd have been making dinner just like this, while I waited for him to come home.

Then jeered at herself for her own sentimentality. Their first home together would have been the penthouse in the glamorous apartment block which Daniel had already occupied, which had its own restaurant, with a delivery service. She wouldn't have been expected to lift a finger. And when they'd eventually set up house, that would have come with a full complement of staff too. Something that would no doubt apply to the house he'd just bought.

She found herself wondering a little wistfully what had happened to the penthouse, recalling how she'd roamed around it open-mouthed the first and only time he'd taken her to see it.

She remembered the sofas like thistledown, the Persian rugs that gleamed like jewels from the vast expanse of polished floor in the living area. She thought of the gleaming bathroom, tiled in a magically misty sea-green, with its enormous tub and the equally spacious shower cabinet. Big enough, she'd told him rapturously, to hold a party in, and had seen his lips twitch.

And most of all she remembered the bedroom. How she'd stood in the doorway, not daring to venture further, and stared speechlessly at the huge bed with its gold silk cover, her mind going into overdrive as the actual implications of being Daniel's wife came home to her as never before.

Because, up to then, physical contact between them during their brief engagement had been almost minimal, she'd realised with bewilderment. He'd held her after—after Simon, but that had been to comfort her. And he'd kissed her when she'd said she'd marry him. There'd been other kisses since—of course there had—but they'd invariably been light—even teasing. Yet she'd found them intensely disturbing nonetheless.

At no time, however, had there been any real pressure from him to change their relationship to a more intimate level. And, in spite of her happiness and longing, she'd been too shy of him, and too conscious of her own inexperience, to initiate any deeper involvement herself.

It had suddenly occurred to her that they were completely alone together, without fear of interruption, and she was sharply, achingly, aware of him standing just behind her.

Her body had tingled as she'd felt the warmth of his nearness, the stir of his breath on her neck, and she'd wished—desperately—crazily—that he'd turn her into his arms and kiss her with passion and desire, as he'd done so often in her imagination. And that he'd lift her and carry her over to the bed, silencing all her doubts and uncertainties for ever as he made love to her.

Maybe that was why he'd brought her there? Because he didn't want to wait any longer. He wanted all of her. Everything she had to give.

And maybe he was only waiting for some sign from her.

She had half turned towards him when she realised just in time that he was moving, stepping backwards away from her. He'd said quietly, almost casually, as he glanced at his watch, 'We should be going.' He'd paused. 'If there's anything about the décor you want to change, you only have to say so.'

And, wrenched by something deeper than disappointment, she'd stammered something inane about the flat being beautiful—perfect. That she wouldn't want to alter a thing.

She supposed he must have sold it at some point after their separation, but why hadn't he acquired something similar—with its own gym, swimming pool and every other convenience known to the mind of man—instead of slumming it here?

So he didn't want to be tied into a long lease? But Daniel Sinclair was a multimillionaire, and could surely dictate his own terms. It made no sense for him to opt merely for this fairly ordinary two-bedroomed job.

She bit her lip. But then Daniel's motives for doing anything would always be a mystery. And she really had to remember that this was none of her business, anyway.

He was here, and he obviously intended to stay, so her reluctant task was to establish some kind of working neutrality. And speculation would simply cloud the issue.

Besides, if she didn't ask any questions she could free herself from any obligation to answer them either.

And maybe the whole wretched subject of the marriage that never was could be finally laid to rest.

Maybe.

Could it really—ever—be that simple? she wondered. And told herself that her eyes were suddenly blurred because she was chopping onions. No other reason could be permitted—or even be possible.

CHAPTER FOUR

IT WASN'T an expensive wine. Neither Jamie nor she had aspired to acquiring a vintage collection, even if they could have afforded it. But it was chilled and crisp, and it soothed the dryness of her throat as Laine, curled up in a corner of the sofa, waited for Daniel's return.

He'd said two hours, but it was now over three. That was, of course, if he planned to return at all. Because it had occurred to her that maybe he'd decided that sharing a roof with her wasn't worth the hassle, and that he was, even at that moment, arranging alternative accommodation somewhere as far away from her as possible.

Which, in the short term, would solve some of her problems, but inevitably create others in their place.

Practically, she could not afford to occupy the flat alone—unlike Jamie, who'd always earned a much larger salary than she'd done, or at least while he'd still been working at Cowper Dymond.

And right now she couldn't actually afford to live in the place at all, she reminded herself unhappily. Thankfully, there was no mortgage to pay, but there were plenty of other bills looming large on the horizon, and if she didn't start earning at once she was going to find herself in real difficulty.

She sighed. As she'd headed home the flat had seemed like a safe refuge. But then investing in Andy's boat had also appeared to be a good deal.

And there had even been a time when the prospect of becoming Daniel's wife had been the answer to her prayers—the fulfilment of her most treasured hopes and dreams.

Oh, God, she thought with sudden anguish, the muscles tightening in her throat. How wrong is it possible to be in one short lifetime?

The sound of his key in the door brought her sharply back to the here and now. She leaned back against the cushions, trying to look perfectly relaxed, but realised at the same time that she was clinging to the stem of her glass as if it was a lifeline.

'Hi.' She forced a smile as he came in, attempting the nonchalant approach, as if she was quite accustomed to his returning from the office for dinner. As she would have been, of course, if their marriage had ever become a reality...

Don't think like that—even for a moment. Don't go there.

'Good evening.' He halted for a moment, studying her, his brows raised sardonically. 'I was quite expecting to find you'd barricaded yourself in during my absence.'

She shrugged, pretending ruefulness. 'The furniture was just too heavy for me to move.' She paused. 'Besides, I talked to Jamie. Found out what had happened.' She shook her head. 'I can't believe he could be such an utter fool.'

'Isn't that rather naïve of you—considering his past record?' Daniel tossed the jacket he was carrying over the back of a chair and loosened his tie, before walking over to one of the shelved alcoves which flanked the fireplace and pouring himself a whisky from the tray of decanters which stood there.

He came back, dropping loose-limbed onto the sofa opposite, and for one sharp, unwary moment she felt the breath catch in her throat.

Hurriedly, she pulled herself together. 'Well—perhaps. But I thought he'd outgrown that—unruly phase. Got his act together.'

'Well, he now has a chance to do exactly that,' he said. 'Perhaps this girl of his can keep him straight. If not, he's on his own next time.'

'You think there'll be one—after this?'

It was his turn to shrug. 'Who knows? Maybe it isn't simply a phase, as you put it, but an extra helping of the Sinclair wild streak and impossible to remove, even with surgery.'

She stared at him. 'What are you talking about? What—streak?'

'This overweening impulse to go looking for danger.' His mouth twisted. 'Simon had it too, remember?'

'I remember nothing of the kind,' Laine said curtly.

'No? Then what took him back to those bloody mountains time after time, constantly pushing himself to go higher—faster—than anyone else?' His voice was harsh. 'And what the hell possessed him to go on that last trip—when everyone tried to talk him out of it?'

She stared down at the pale gold of her wine, her throat tightening. 'I don't know,' she said in a low voice. 'I've never known.'

'Exactly,' he said.

Her gaze met his with swift defiance. 'Well, please don't include me in this absurd generalisation about my family. I certainly don't go looking for trouble.'

'But you seem to find it, all the same,' he said unanswerably. 'How's the ankle?'

'Better,' she returned. 'I found some more bandages in the bathroom cupboard and strapped it up again, all ready for my trek to the job centre tomorrow.'

'I'm pleased to hear it,' Daniel said smoothly. 'And you appear to have been busy in other ways.' He glanced towards the kitchen. 'Something smells good.'

'You cleared Jamie's room for me, so I've cooked dinner for you.' She paused. 'Chicken *puttanesca*. I hope you like it.'

'Thank you, but sadly we'll never know.' There was no trace of regret in his tone. 'I'm going out tonight. I merely came back to change.'

'Hot date?' She kept her voice light, faintly amused, ignoring the ludicrous, unreasoning disappointment that speared her.

'Is there any other kind?'

'Serious?'

He swallowed some of his whisky, watching her steadily. 'Is that really any of your business?'

'Well, yes, in a way,' Laine countered. 'I just wonder—if the pair of you are an item—why you don't move in with the lady instead of living here? It would seem to make more sense—that's all.'

His glance was cynical. 'It's not that serious.'

'Poor girl.'

'She can take care of herself,' he returned curtly. 'Speaking of which, this could be a good time to get something straight. Put some guidelines in place. Because we're not playing happy families here, Laine. You're not Si's little sister any more. And I'm not your surrogate brother.'

He added icily, 'Also, in case you've forgotten, you lost any right you ever had to enquire into my private life two years ago.'

He allowed her a moment to digest that, then went on, 'We share this flat, but we maintain our own space at all times. So, if I intend to be here for a meal I'll let you know, and we'll make some arrangement about the use of the kitchen. But we both cook for ourselves, and there'll be no cosying-up round the stove. Understood?'

'Of course,' she said tautly, aware that her face had warmed. 'Although *cosy* is never a word I'd associate with you. And I'll make very sure that I repay you for the food I've used this evening.'

He said wearily, 'Don't be so damned absurd. I'm not actually begrudging you a meal. Just don't make a habit of it.'

His firm mouth tightened. 'This is not a situation either of us would have chosen, Laine, but it exists, and we must make the best of it. And we do that by going our own ways and leading our own lives. Right?' He added, 'After all, you were the one who said privacy should be respected.'

He waited until she slowly nodded, then finished his whisky and got to his feet, taking the glass into the kitchen. She heard the faint rattle as he put it in the dishwasher.

It all seemed so normal—so domestic, she thought. Except, of course, that it was just the opposite. This was a battleground, and she had to make damned sure she wasn't a casualty. Not again.

On his way back Daniel paused momentarily, looking down at her, the hazel eyes hard.

'By the way,' he added, his voice soft but not gentle, 'please don't bother to wait up for me—tonight or any other night.'

And he went across to his room and closed the door, leaving her staring after him from her corner of the sofa as if she'd been frozen there.

Laine was at the stove, draining the pasta to go with the chicken, when she heard the faint slam of the flat door, signalling his departure.

And goodnight and goodbye to you, too, she thought, grinding black pepper over her *penne* as if she was twisting someone's throat.

Much of her earlier appetite seemed to have deserted her, but she forced herself to eat at least some of her solitary meal, sitting at the breakfast bar in the kitchen, rather than at the elegant circular dining table in the living room.

I'd feel silly in there on my own, she thought. But I'd have felt an even bigger fool if I'd used the silverware and the crystal and set two places.

Jamie had told her to be nice, but it was difficult to see how that was to be achieved now that her first awkward attempt at *rapprochement* had been so signally rejected.

But maybe that was for the best too—under the circumstances.

You're not Si's little sister any more. Words which told her quite unequivocally—even brutally—that there was nothing left, not even a residual fondness. And certainly none of the reluctant sense of obligation that had led to their marriage.

He'd totally shrugged off his unwanted responsibilities and reclaimed his freedom. At the same time coldly emphasising that Daniel wanted the woman she'd become no more than he'd desired the girl she'd once been.

And that from now on she was on her own in every conceivable way.

Her heart felt like a stone in her chest. It had never occurred to her even for a moment that she could find herself in this impossible situation. All along she'd had just one simple plan—never to be alone with him again. There was no alternative scheme—no fall-back position—because she'd believed with painful confidence that they'd never be necessary.

Yet here she was, she thought wretchedly. Trapped and, for the foreseeable future anyway, helpless.

If it had been the same for him she could perhaps have steeled herself to bear it. Learned to move about in their shared space as if she was tiptoeing on eggshells. Taught herself to edge round him—live on some perimeter of this joint existence.

But the fact was that he didn't care. Because she didn't matter enough to make him do so. She'd once been a burden, now she was no more than a nuisance—a vague irritant in the smooth running of his life. Nothing more.

All the pain, the tears, the stumbling days and sleepless nights, and the yawning desolation of loneliness had been hers alone.

And just the knowledge of that was the kind of anguish she'd prayed she would never feel again.

An anguish she could never let him see in the weeks that stretched ahead. Because she wasn't sure which would be worse to endure—his indifference or his pity.

She swallowed thickly, pushing her plate away, and slid off the stool. Don't think, she told herself. Keep busy.

She worked like a robot, stacking the dishwasher and selecting a programme, then placing the extra chicken with its thick, aromatic sauce in a covered dish in the fridge, to provide her with her next evening meal, before tidying the kitchen and restoring the stove and surfaces to their earlier pristine gleam.

Making certain she'd leave no trace of her presence for him to complain about there either, she told herself with cold resolve.

It was a long evening. Laine tried watching television, but she soon realised she'd grown completely out of touch with current programming, and found herself flicking restlessly from channel to channel, searching for something that might grip her interest.

In the end she gave up in exasperation, and decided to read instead. There were some books on the alcove shelves that were new to her—most of them thrillers that she guessed had been acquired by Jamie, and each of them triumphantly claiming to be 'the new number-one bestseller'.

They can't all be that, surely? she thought, pulling a face as she picked the least overtly lurid. But the story failed to engage her particularly, and the identity of the villain seemed all too obvious even by chapter three, so, sighing, she abandoned that as well.

One of the things she'd managed to rescue from the boat was her address book, and she sat slowly turning over the pages, trying to summon up the courage to ring someone—anyone. Fiona from the gallery, perhaps? Or Celia Welton, her best friend from school, who'd been her bridesmaid at that ill-fated wedding.

At the same time she knew full well that she wouldn't be doing so—or not yet, anyway. Because she wasn't ready to face the inevitable questions—especially when it emerged that she and Daniel were back sharing a roof.

She'd been let off the hook when their marriage had ended with such startling suddenness, because people had recognised that she was in desperate pain, and suppressed their natural curiosity and concern, standing back to allow her to recover. Celia, in particular, bewildered but loyal and kind, had helped picked up the pieces.

But this new development would require answers that simply weren't possible immediately.

Because she was still in shock. She needed time to think things through. To come up with some feasible explanation for everything that had happened to her. And make it clear that sharing a flat with Daniel was not the basis for some kind of re-conciliation—and never would be.

She swallowed. Which meant, in turn, that at some point she

might be asked about what had happened two years earlier. Why her marriage hadn't survived the honeymoon, or even the wedding night, given the bleak significance of that swift annulment. Because after this length of time, tact would not be a primary consideration any longer.

And if they did ask, what the hell could she say? she wondered wearily. Certainly not the truth.

And if she tried saying that she'd realised she didn't love him no one would believe her for a moment. She'd worn her heart on her sleeve too openly and for too long for that.

She didn't even know when it had begun. When Daniel had stopped being just Simon's friend, and the surrogate brother he'd alluded to so acidly, and occupied a very different role in her hopes and dreams.

But she could remember very clearly her first half-term at Randalls, when everyone else had gone home for the weekend, being told kindly by the matron that a visitor was coming to take her out to tea.

Simon, she'd thought joyfully. It had to be Simon. But she'd been wrong, because it had been Daniel who had waited in the front hall as she came down the stairs, her heart thundering in nervous excitement.

'What are you doing here?'

'I went down to Abbotsbrook to see you, and you weren't there.'

'No,' she said. 'It wasn't convenient this time. Mummy had other people coming to stay.'

He nodded. 'So I gathered. Therefore, I decided to pay you a visit here instead.'

'But you shouldn't have,' she whispered, looking anxiously around. 'It's against the rules. We're only allowed out with immediate family. Mrs Hallam is terribly strict about that. Is Simon with you?'

'No, he's off to the Cairngorms, climbing.' He pulled a face. 'The ruling passion, once again. I'm here in his place.'

'Didn't you want to go with him?' she asked shyly. Simon

might not be here, she thought, but neither was the horrible
Candida. The Daniel she knew was back, and she wanted to turn
a cartwheel in sheer joy.

'God, no.' He shuddered. 'I get vertigo if I climb a ladder.
Now, are you coming out to tea, or not? It's all fixed. We have
your principal's blessing.'

'But how? I don't understand.'

'Friends in high places, sweetheart.' He swept her out to the
long, low sports car waiting on the drive. 'My father just happens
to be on the board of governors. Mrs H can refuse me nothing.
Anyway, I want to know how you're getting on.'

Over sandwiches, scones with jam and cream, and rich chocolate cake served in the hushed and luxurious environs of a nearby
country house hotel, she told him everything, her face glowing.
Told him about the challenge of the work, her favourite teachers,
the ghastly savoury mince served on Mondays that she hated, the
friends she'd already made, and the possibility that next term she
might get into the junior swimming team.

'And Celia Welton has asked her mother if I can stay with
them during the Christmas holidays,' she ended in triumph,
adding breathlessly, 'Coming here is the best thing that's ever
happened to me.'

'Well,' he said lightly, and smiled at her across the teatime
debris. 'That's all right, then.'

Rules and regulations notwithstanding, his visits had become
a regular and anticipated feature of her life at Randalls, and
Laine had soon found herself being quizzed about him by some
of the senior girls, who tended to be much in evidence when he
was expected.

'A kind of brother?' one of them had echoed enviously after
her stumbling explanation. 'Daniel Flynn, no less. My God, I
should be so lucky. Sex on legs, and rich with it.'

Was that when it had started—when her ideas about him
had begun to change? Perhaps. All she could remember, as
she'd progressed into her teens, was suddenly finding herself

awkward and tongue-tied whenever he was around. Fantasising about him in ways she was ashamed to recall. Longing desperately to see him, but crippled with shyness when he appeared.

And eventually, unable to deal with the confused riot of emotion inside her, making excuses not to see him at all—citing too much work, an extra games practice. She had not, of course, been able to totally avoid him at Abbotsbrook, where she'd had less control over the matter.

But when he'd been there, he'd had little time to spare for her, anyway. When he and Simon had visited they'd invariably been on their way somewhere else, and accompanied by an ever-changing—and interchangeable—series of girls, usually blonde. Laine had privately and contemptuously dismissed them as 'The Clones', even while she had secretly bitten her nails down to the quick with the most savage and primitive form of jealousy, and despised herself for it.

But that had by no means been her only problem. Her mother had become more anxious about money, and more discontented all the time, and her complaints had made Laine feel embarrassed and inadequate.

'You'd think Simon would help out more,' Angela had said bitterly on that last occasion. 'I thought that's why he'd abandoned his plan to join the Forestry Commission and taken that job at the bank.'

Laine said nothing. She knew how much it had cost Simon to give up his cherished dream and work in the City instead. Small wonder he was devoting so much of his free time to his beloved climbing, she thought. He was now becoming known as a mountaineer, and had already been on a number of expeditions to the Alps and the Dolomites. But Laine knew that his sights were set on more distant horizons than that, and it worried her a little.

And, on a more personal level, Simon was causing her concern too.

'I'm having dinner with an old friend,' he'd told her casually a few months earlier, when he'd visited her at school. 'Remember Candy, who used to date Daniel years ago?'

'Yes,' Laine had said quietly. 'I remember.' And had crossed her fingers that it would stop at dinner.

But it hadn't. And it seemed that each time Laine went home Candy was there, all smiles and charm, cooing over Angela, praising the house, and rhapsodising over Graham Sinclair's books.

'I had no idea Simon was related to *that* Sinclair,' she'd enthused. 'My God, I'm such a fan.'

Laine had been tempted to ask which of the novels she liked best, certain that she hadn't read any of them, but had controlled the impulse.

'Mum,' she said, one evening when they were alone. 'Is it serious, do you think, this Simon and Candy thing?'

Her mother put down her magazine. 'It's certainly going that way. They're talking about an engagement. Why do you ask?'

'It just seems odd—when she was Dan's girlfriend originally.'

Angela laughed indulgently. 'My dear child, that was *years* ago, and a lot of water's flowed under the bridge since then. Dan is very wealthy, of course, especially now that his father is dead, and he has charm to spare, but I think Candy knew quite early in their relationship that it was going nowhere.

'And Dan certainly lost no time in replacing her many times over, so he was hardly heartbroken when they split. In fact, I understand that it's all been very civilised, and he may well be best man at the wedding.'

She paused. 'It doesn't matter to you, surely, that she was once Dan's girlfriend? For God's sake, Elaine, tell me you're not still harbouring that ridiculous childhood crush where he's concerned. Because that would be too sad—and horribly embarrassing.'

'No,' Laine said quietly. 'I don't have a crush on Daniel Flynn.'

Although perhaps that's how I should have tried to see it—before it was too late, Laine thought now, leaning back and closing her eyes, wearily. As the kind of worship I'd have probably given a film star or a rock musician in other circumstances. Something transient that I could look back on one day and smile.

Instead, I made him the sun in my sky. The centre of my universe. The focus of everything I wanted from life. And that made me—vulnerable. Especially when I was seventeen and came face to face with my first personal tragedy.

She'd had no presentiment that anything was going to happen. Her only real foreboding had concerned Simon and Candy's wedding, which had been scheduled to take place in the summer. And for which she would be required to wear lavender taffeta.

But, quite apart from that, she had known in her heart that Candy was the last person in the world she'd have chosen as a sister-in-law. And suspected the feeling was mutual.

Their only common ground was the vexed subject of Simon's climbing. Candy had been uneasy about it and so had she—especially when he'd been invited at the last minute to go to Annapurna in place of someone who was ill.

'It's the chance of a lifetime,' he'd said buoyantly. 'Serious stuff. A dream come true.' His face had clouded slightly. 'But I've promised Candy that I'll cut down once we're married. She says it's no longer a hobby but an obsession, and she could be right.'

Laine swallowed, remembering how she'd been sent for by the headmistress, and had gone to her study filled with trepidation, wondering what she'd done to fall from grace. But Mrs Hallam's expression had spoken of distress rather than severity, and she'd risen and came round the desk, taking Laine's hands in hers. An unheard-of gesture.

'My dear,' she said gravely. 'I'm afraid I have some very sad news for you.' She hesitated, shaking her head sorrowfully, and Laine thought, *Daniel—oh, please God, don't let anything have happened to Daniel.*

'What—is it?' She hardly recognised her own voice.

'Elaine, dear, there is no easy way to say this. It's—your

brother—Simon. There's been an accident, and he and another man have been killed.'

'Simon?' Shock mingled with shame that her first thought—her instinctive prayer—had been about Daniel. 'Oh, no—please. There must be some mistake.'

Mrs Hallam bent her head. 'Laine—I'm so sorry.'

She heard herself give a little moan, and was gently encouraged to sit in one of the armchairs normally reserved for visitors, told that tea had been sent for, and that matron was packing a case for her, because her brother was expected at some time during the next hour to take her home.

'Would you like a friend—Celia, perhaps—to sit with you until he arrives?'

'No, thank you. I—I think I'd rather be alone. If that's all right.'

And Mrs Hallam nodded and quietly withdrew.

A member of the kitchen staff brought the tea, poured it out for her, and pressed the cup and saucer into her hands.

Where they remained, the tea cold and untouched, half an hour later, when the study door opened and Daniel came in.

She stood up, spilling some of the liquid on her skirt. She said numbly, 'It's you. I—I thought Jamie was coming.'

'He was, but your mother became hysterical at the idea of being left.'

He took the cup and saucer from her shaking hand and replaced them on the tray. He said gently, 'They've put your case in my car, Laine. We can go as soon as you feel able.'

She shook her head. 'I don't seem to—feel anything at all. Not yet. You see, I—I can't quite believe it.'

'No one can.'

She stared down at the carpet. 'What happened—do you know?'

He said quietly, 'Details are sketchy, but it seems there was some kind of rock fall, and he and an Italian guy were swept away.'

'Oh, God,' she whispered, horrified.

'Si had named Jamie as next of kin, and he was the one they notified before the newscasts went out. He was meeting your mother for lunch. She'd gone up to London to do some shopping with Candida, and he asked me to go with him to break the news.' He was silent for a moment. 'It was—truly bad. One of the worst moments of my life.'

He sighed. 'Jamie drove them down to Abbotsbrook, and the doctor's seen them and prescribed sedatives. But your mother still wouldn't let Jamie out of her sight.'

'I can hardly blame her for that.' She swallowed. 'I'm ready to leave now.'

They had been travelling for twenty minutes when she said, in a small stifled voice, 'Could you stop, please? I think I'm going to be sick.'

Daniel pulled over onto the verge and she stumbled out, kneeling on the short grass, her shoulders hunched as she retched dryly and painfully over and over again, until at last the harsh sounds became gasping sobs, and tears followed.

He lifted her and held her close, his hand cupping the back of her head as she wept into his shoulder in a fierce, cleansing outpouring of grief.

Cry while you can, an icy voice in her brain seemed to be saying, even as she clung to him. But do it here and now. Because when you get to Abbotsbrook you'll have to provide comfort to your mother, and the girl who was nearly Simon's widow. And you'll have to sort Jamie out too.

At last, when there seemed to be no tears left, she leaned against him, trembling a little, knowing that she did not want to move out of the warmth of his embrace.

He was the first to detach himself, holding her deliberately away from him as he looked down at her pale, unhappy face. He said quietly, 'We have to get back. People will be waiting for us.'

He retrieved a bottle of mineral water from the cool box in the boot and made her drink most of it, before damping his handkerchief with the remainder and wiping away the worst of the tearstains.

'You're going to need all your strength, Laine,' he told her almost abruptly as he started the engine. 'These next few days are not going to be easy.'

If you would only hold me, she thought, I could face anything. Even—this.

But she said nothing, sitting beside him in silence for the rest of the journey.

When they arrived at Abbotsbrook, Daniel carried her bag into the house and set it down in the hall.

'I have things to do, Laine.' His voice sounded almost curt. 'I'll be back later.'

She watched him go, controlling an impulse to run after him. Beg him not to leave her. Because she had to be strong, she thought. Starting now.

As she heard the car's engine die away someone said her name, and she saw Jamie emerging from the drawing room, his face pale and set.

He came over and gave her an awkward hug. 'God, sis, I can't believe it, can you? I keep thinking that I'm going to wake up at any moment, and find it's all been a bad dream.' He looked past her. 'Where's Dan? They've both been asking for him.'

'He had to go.' She hesitated. 'Jamie, I don't want to seem heartless, but wouldn't it be better if Candida could be looked after by her own family? We're going to have our hands full.'

'I suggested it, naturally, but it seems she doesn't get on with her mother.' He shook his head. 'The drive down was a nightmare. She kept saying that Annapurna was cursed, and she'd known something dreadful was going to happen. You can imagine the effect that had on Ma,' he added heavily.

She nodded. 'Is she using Simon's room?'

'Well, yes. She just walked in there and shut the door. I—didn't know what to say. After all, it's where she's always slept when she's stayed here, I suppose.'

She sighed. 'I suppose so too—and yet...' She patted his shoulder. 'I'll go and sit with Mother. Wait for her to wake up.'

And wait for Dan to come back too. Because he was Simon's

best friend, and for that reason, if no other, he'll be here for us. Or for a while, at least. Until the mourning time is over, and we all pick up our lives again somehow.

She did not dare look any further into the future than that. Because she knew it would be like staring down into an abyss. A terrible place that she had never known existed until this moment. But which seemed, somehow, to have been waiting for her the whole of her life.

CHAPTER FIVE

SHE moved at last, slowly and stiffly, wondering just how long she'd been sitting there, staring into space. Knowing, however, that it was getting late, and that she had no wish to be found hanging round like a cobweb in the corner when Daniel returned.

On the other hand, she felt too much on edge to guarantee she was going to get the night's sleep she so badly needed. She had embarked on a long and painful journey, she thought with a pang, and it was not finished yet. Not by any means.

But once it was over, and the past had finally been laid to rest, she might be able to find peace—of a kind.

In the short term, something soothing to drink might help, she decided, trailing into the kitchen. Perhaps Mrs Evershott's tried and trusted remedy for insomnia would be the answer.

She heated milk and poured it into a beaker, adding a spoonful of honey and a grating of nutmeg, wondering, as she did so, what had happened to the housekeeper who'd looked after them all for so long. Hoping that she'd found a family who would value her as she deserved, and not become another casualty of the upheaval that had affected all their lives.

She took the beaker into the room she would now have to think of as hers, and sipped the milk slowly as she prepared for bed. Her final action before she climbed under the covers was to return her address book to her bag.

It would be far better at this stage simply to keep quiet about her return, she told herself. To find a job, keep her head down, and wait for Daniel to finish refurbishing his property and move out before she made contact with any old friends.

It would not be for long, she told herself. Nothing lasted for ever—not joy, not grief, perhaps not love either—and this present situation would also pass—eventually.

She might even be able to make a joke of it. *It was hideously awkward, of course. And as he was leaving we agreed it was just as well we didn't stay married, or we'd have surely killed each other.*

Or she could be terribly casual and civilised instead. *No, it wasn't really a problem. We were always friends, you know, long before the marriage thing. And now we're friends again, so it worked out well, in a funny way.*

It might be better not to mention it at all. Pretend it had never happened.

She stifled a sigh. She would decide on her approach as and when it became necessary. And for the time being she had other priorities.

Switching off the lamp, she turned on her side and tried to relax. To compose herself for sleep. But her mind was relentlessly awake and buzzing with images.

With memories as sharp and painful as a knife wound.

Simon's body, and that of his climbing partner Carlo Marchetti, had never been recovered—even though Daniel had travelled out to the base camp with offers of money and resources to spearhead a renewed search—so it had been a memorial service rather than a funeral that had taken place at their local parish church.

And the days leading up to it had been just as bad as Daniel had warned, or even worse, with Laine's own grieving process having to be put on hold while she supported her mother through this crisis.

And not just her mother. Because Candida had seemed to take up residence, as if she was Simon's widow, and Laine had begun to wonder if she had any plans to leave.

At the service Angela had looked ethereal, in a new and expensive black velvet coat, as she'd walked, with Jamie, down the aisle of the crowded church to the front pew. Candida had followed, clinging to Daniel's arm, thus ensuring that Laine was left to bring up the rear.

Many of the mourners had come back to the house afterwards, and Laine had been kept busy helping Mrs Evershott offer sherry and other refreshments, while her mother had drooped on the sofa, with Candida in close attendance.

And when everyone had gone, it had been time for another ritual—the reading of Simon's will.

It had been made hurriedly, just before his departure, and he'd only had one thing of real value to bequeath—a flat in Mannion Place, London, which he'd inherited from his father, and left jointly to Jamie and Laine, together with the accruing rent from the flat's sitting tenants, a Mr and Mrs Beaumont.

'What is this nonsense?' Angela was suddenly wilting no longer, but sitting bolt upright, her eyes blazing. 'That property was part of my husband's estate. I always understood Simon was to have a life interest only. So it should have reverted to me.'

Mr Hawthorn, the family solicitor, had coughed dryly. 'No, it was an outright bequest, Mrs Sinclair, and your son was entitled to dispose of it as he saw fit. And his brother and sister are his sole beneficiaries.'

Even in the depth of her bewilderment at this turn of events, Laine was suddenly conscious of Candida's white face and set mouth, and realised that Simon's last wishes had not mentioned her either.

Daniel had deliberately stayed away from the reading, and eventually Laine went in search of him, thankful to escape from the house for a while. She found him at the end of the garden, standing on the bank of the river, skimming stones across the surface of the water, his face grim. She said his name with a touch of uncertainty and he turned to look at her, with no lightening of his expression.

'Is there something you want?'

She tried to smile. 'Just to get away for a while.' She paused. 'I suppose you know about Simon's legacy?'

It was Dan's turn to hesitate. 'He mentioned it—yes. You should be pleased. I gather it's a valuable piece of real estate.'

'It must be,' she said. 'Judging by the tide of ill-feeling running at the moment.' She bit her lip. 'My mother is suggesting that Jamie and I should refuse the bequest and pass the flat, and its rent, over to her.'

'Well, Jamie must make up his own mind,' he said flatly. 'But fortunately any decision is out of your hands until you're eighteen. And at present I imagine your trustees will take a very different view of the matter.'

'Maybe Si should have left the flat to Candida,' she said slowly. 'After all, she was going to be his wife, and she gets nothing,' she added, hating herself for not caring more. 'I suppose he assumed he'd be coming back, and could change things later.'

He turned back to the river. 'Yes,' he said harshly. 'I believe that's exactly what he thought.'

'It's so awful without him,' she said, in a small, subdued voice. 'Everything's such a mess.'

'More than you know.' He spoke the words half under his breath, then forced a faint smile as she looked at him in bewilderment. 'But you'll soon be out of it, Laine. After all, you'll be going back to Randalls in a few days.'

'Yes,' she said. 'Is it very dreadful of me to wish I was there now?'

'No,' he said quietly. 'I don't think so. I think Si would understand completely.'

There was another silence, then she said, 'The boat's there,' nodding towards the elderly dinghy. She added wistfully, 'Do you think we might go out in it—for old times' sake?'

'No time, I'm afraid.' His voice was crisp and cool. 'I have to be leaving. I fly to Sydney tomorrow, and I have some stuff to collate before I go.'

'Oh,' she said, struggling to hide her disappointment. 'I see. Yes, of course. And I'd better go back too. They'll be wondering where I am.' She hesitated again. 'Dan—about the flat. Someone should talk to Mother—calm her down like Simon used to do.' She swallowed. 'I suppose you couldn't…?'

'Too damned right.' There was real anger in his voice. 'Get it into your head, Laine. I am not Simon, and I can't take his place— even if I wanted to. Besides, he couldn't divert your mother once she'd really got her teeth stuck into a grievance. You know that.'

'I suppose so.' She sighed. 'I don't know what to do.'

'Then do nothing,' he said. 'She'll get over it. You concentrate on passing your exams and going off to university next year. You have a career to plan—a future—a whole life. You have to let your mother go her own way, for better or worse.'

'I'm sorry.' *She was more than sorry. She was mortified.* 'I didn't mean to impose.'

He said more gently, 'And I didn't mean to snap. Maybe a few weeks in Australia will bring me back in a better temper.'

Just as long as it brings you back…

He paused, looking down at her, and for a dizzy moment she thought he was going to touch her cheek. Or even—kiss her. And almost—for one infinitesimal moment—she swayed towards him.

But instead he said quietly, 'Things will improve with time, Laine. Believe me.' And walked quickly away.

But he was wrong, Laine thought, twisting restlessly and trying to fight her pillow into a more manageable shape. As she had so soon found out.

It had been three days later, on her return from the village, where she'd been posting another batch of replies to the letters of condolence, that she'd sought out her mother in the drawing room.

She said, 'I've just found my school trunk in the hall. What's going on? How did it get here?'

Angela was sitting on the sofa, glancing through a fashion magazine. She said, 'I had it sent for. See that it's unpacked, please. It's terribly in the way.'

'But why?' Laine stared at her. 'It's nowhere near the end of term, and I have stacks of coursework to catch up with. I can't afford any more time off.'

'And I can't afford any more of the expense of keeping you at that school.' Angela put down the magazine and looked up at her daughter. 'Therefore I telephoned to Mrs Hallam and said you would not be returning to Randalls because from now on you were needed at home. She quite understood.'

'Which is more than I do.' Laine swallowed. 'Mother, my fees are paid from the bursary—unless it's been withdrawn for some reason. Has it?'

'Not as far as I'm aware. But it doesn't cover everything. Think of all the items of uniform I've had to replace, as well as the extras—your piano lessons, for instance. It simply can't go on.'

Laine felt suddenly very cold. 'But I have to go back to school. How else am I going to get to university?'

'I'm afraid you're not.' Her mother sounded almost brisk. 'I've only just finished subsidising Jamie, and I've no intention of starting again with you. Anyway, I have to consider the running costs of this house, and now that Simon is no longer here to help with the finances savings have to be made.'

She paused. 'I have therefore decided to let Mrs Evershott go, and we will have to manage the housework and cooking between us.'

'You're sacking Evvy?' Laine was aghast. 'But you can't.'

'I've already done so,' Angela said shortly. 'While she's working out her notice you'll spend time with her, learning how to run the house. Don't forget it was only last term that I paid a small fortune for you to go on that cookery course in Normandy,' she added acidly. 'I only hope it was money well-spent. At any rate, it's high time you made yourself useful round here.'

Laine's heart sank like a stone. 'Please,' she said. 'Please say you don't mean this.' She swallowed. 'We're talking about my life, here.'

'And what about *my* life?' There was a sudden strident note in her mother's voice. 'Do you realise what it's been like for me since your father died? The way I've been stuck down here— having to coax people down to stay three weekends out of four to avoid going mad with boredom?'

She got to her feet, walking restlessly round the room. 'This house has been nothing but a burden for years—and it's a burden you're going to share, Elaine, or at least until you're eighteen.'

She paused, then added brusquely, 'Ask Mrs Evershott for some plastic bags for your school uniform. You won't be needing any of it again, and it can go with the rest of the rubbish tomorrow.'

Laine watched her return to her seat and reach for the magazine again. Then she moved, slowly and stiffly, crossing to the door and closing it quietly behind her. She stood for a moment in the hallway, feeling stunned—battered—as if Angela had hit her, knocking her to the floor.

She supposed she'd always known instinctively that she wasn't her mother's favourite, but if she'd hoped that they would somehow be drawn closer in their mourning for Simon she now realised how mistaken she was.

I feel as if I don't know her, she thought. As if I've spent my whole life living with a stranger.

Yet, looking back, she could see the resentment had always been there, never far from the surface. But not targeting her—or not openly—and certainly not until then.

However, she soon realised she was not the only sufferer, when she made her reluctant way to the kitchen and saw Mrs Evershott's white face and compressed lips.

'Oh, Evvy.' Distressed, she put her arms round the older woman's rigid figure and hugged her. 'I'm so sorry.

'I would never have believed it,' the housekeeper said tone-lessly. 'Never credited that Mrs Sinclair could treat me like this after all these years.' She swallowed. 'It would never have happened, Miss Laine, if poor Mr Simon had been spared. Never.'

Along with so much else, Laine thought, as she lay, staring

sightlessly into the darkness. And especially, crucially, her brief and bitter marriage.

All the demons were out of the box now, tormenting her wincing mind. Reminding her, with merciless precision, of everything that had happened in those bleak, bewildering weeks, when she'd gone from a girl with all her hopes and dreams in front of her to being a glorified domestic servant.

There had been nights at first when she had fallen into bed exhausted from the non-stop cooking and cleaning and her mother's incessant demands. But she'd been young and strong, and eventually she had established a workable routine largely drawn from her predecessor's neatly compiled roster of household tasks.

And in the middle of it all she had become eighteen years old. There had been no party—Angela had said tearfully that it was too soon for any celebration—but Celia and some of Laine's other friends had driven over from Randalls at the weekend and taken her out for a meal in Market Lambton, followed by a visit to its only nightclub, and for a few hours she'd been able to hide her unhappiness behind a shield of music and laughter.

On her actual birthday she had received a watch from her mother, an iPod from Jamie, and a surprise parcel from her late grandmother, sent on by the trustees, which contained Mrs Sinclair's pearls and her copy of Tennyson's *Idylls of the King*, complete with the legend of Lancelot and Elaine.

And also out of the blue had come a messengered bouquet of eighteen pink roses from Daniel, with a velvet box tucked in among them holding a pair of gold earrings, shaped like flowers, with a tiny diamond at each centre.

'Charming,' Angela commented with a touch of acidity, as Laine shyly showed them off over dinner. 'But surely a little over the top for a child of your age.'

Jamie leaned forward, his gaze flicking from his mother's raised brows to Candida's faint scowl, and smiled. 'On the contrary,' he drawled. 'Maybe Dan's giving us all a salutary reminder that Lainie's now officially a woman. And entitled to a life of her own,' he added pointedly. 'Together with the ability to make decisions about it.'

There was an odd silence, then, 'Oh, don't be absurd,' Angela said shortly, and turned the conversation to other topics, leaving Laine wondering, and even a little uneasy.

Yet nothing could have prepared her for the bombshell that had exploded a few days later, or its implications for her future.

And for which, even now, she was still experiencing the fallout.

She turned over, punching her pillow into submission, then burying her face in it. Telling herself to relax, because everything would seem better after a good night's sleep, but knowing at the same time that it wasn't true.

That the pain would still be there waiting for her when she opened her eyes.

It was very early when she awoke next morning, and she lay for a moment, totally disorientated, listening to the distant hum of city traffic as opposed to the creak of a boat at anchor.

Her eyes felt as if they were full of sand, and her throat was equally dry—almost as if she'd been crying in her sleep, making her glad she could not remember her dreams.

She glanced at the illuminated dial of her bedside clock and sat up, pushing her hair back from her face. She had a full day ahead of her, she reminded herself, and turning over for another doze was a luxury she couldn't afford.

She bathed and put on her underwear, then looked along the wardrobe rail for job-hunting gear. However limited her options, she needed to make the most of them, which meant looking neat and efficient, she thought, pulling out a black skirt and another of her white cotton shirts. Both were clean, but creased, demanding a short stint at the ironing board before they presented the correct image.

Belted into her robe, she opened her door cautiously and peeped into the living room, but everything in the flat seemed quiet and completely still. And long may it remain so, Laine thought, as she trod silently on bare feet to the tall built-in kitchen cupboard where the iron was stored. Especially as it seemed Daniel now chose to sleep with his bedroom door slightly ajar for some reason and, accordingly, she needed to keep the noise level down.

Her task accomplished, she was creeping back to her room, with the freshly pressed garments over her arm, when it suddenly occurred to her that Daniel's door was open because that was how he'd left it when he went out the previous evening.

And that could only mean...

She swallowed convulsively, the clothes crushed against her as if they were some form of defence, as she told herself that, whether he was there or not, it was none of her business. That it could not be allowed to matter to her one way or the other. And, that for her own peace of mind, it was much better not to know.

She was still telling herself all this as the door gave easily to her hand, affording her a perfect view of the empty room, and the wide, smooth bed, with its unruffled covers. Providing absolute confirmation, if it had ever been needed, that Daniel had spent the night somewhere else entirely.

So now you know, she told herself stonily. And what good has it done you?

You're not married to him, and you never were—not in the real sense of the word. Which was your own decision. No one else's. And you're quite well aware that he's not going to sleep alone just because you turned him away. You've been aware of it for two whole years, so you should be used to it by now.

He's not your husband, and he never was, so it's ludicrous to feel like this. To feel sick—hurt—betrayed, as if he's been unfaithful to you. To allow jealousy to rip through you like a poisoned claw. To imagine him with another woman, making love, sharing with her everything that you could have had, but that you deliberately denied yourself.

She said aloud, 'I can't let this happen. I can't think like this and stay sane. So I have to close myself off—to become, in effect, blind, deaf and dumb while the present situation endures.

'And when it's finally over, and he's gone, I can let myself deal with it and begin to feel again. To become, at last, a whole person. 'Somehow…'

A few hours later she had a job—although not without a certain reluctance on the part of her new employer.

'You're very young to be a Citi-Clean operative,' Mrs Moss commented, looking at Laine over her glasses. 'We usually prefer more mature ladies. Our clients are all professional people, and they demand high standards.' She shook her head. 'You don't seem the type, Miss Sinclair.'

Laine gave her an equable smile. 'I assure you, I'm quite used to hard work.'

'Well, I've had two of my best girls leave recently, so I'm short-staffed at the moment. I suppose it wouldn't hurt to give you a month's trial,' the older woman said grudgingly. 'I supply uniforms, and all cleaning materials, and I don't expect them to be wasted. Also, I'll need two character references. I'm very strict about that. After all, most of our work is done in the absence of the client.'

She ran quickly through the wages, which were reasonable, and the hours, which were long, adding, 'You'll be paired with Denise—she's one of my most experienced staff. She'll assess you, and report back to me.'

Her gaze went down to Laine's strapped ankle, and she pursed her lips dubiously. 'Cleaning is physically demanding, Miss Sinclair. I hope you're strong enough to stand up to it?'

'A slight wrench,' Laine told her. 'It will be fine by Monday.'

Mrs Moss sniffed. 'Then I'll expect you to report here at seven thirty a.m. And I require punctuality.'

I don't think, Laine reflected as she left the Citi-Clean office, that Mrs Moss and I are destined to be friends. But what the hell? I'm not qualified to do much else, and it's not a lifetime commitment.

However, she promised herself, once these next difficult weeks are over, I can start to make some real plans.

She celebrated her return to the workplace by going into a small café, and treating herself to one of its massive all-day breakfasts, complete with a mountain of toast and a pot of very strong tea, courtesy of the Sinclair Rescue Fund. She'd been putting the iron away earlier when she'd suddenly remembered the old coffee jar, hidden behind the cleaning materials, where she and Jamie had kept spare cash for any domestic emergencies that might arise.

She had told herself that Jamie would almost certainly have emptied it before he left, but he must have forgotten it too, or been in too much of a hurry, because she'd found an unbelievable sixty pounds tucked away there, which, with care, would take care of her most pressing needs.

It would certainly spare her a visit to the bank, which, she recalled, biting her lip, had totally opposed her investment in the boat charter business, and advised most stringently against it. They probably wouldn't say I told you so, but they'd almost certainly regard her as a bad risk until she could prove she'd stabilised her finances.

And it would also save her the ultimate humiliation of having to ask for help from Daniel—especially as he'd offered a financial settlement at the time of their separation which her lawyer had described as 'astonishingly generous—under the circumstances', and which she, wounded to the heart by those same circumstances, had turned down flat.

She'd added curtly, 'Please tell Mr Flynn that I want nothing from him except the ending of the marriage. Not now. Not ever.'

And that, she thought, had been the last contact between them, even at third hand, until the horror of yesterday. It was also something Daniel was unlikely to have forgiven—or forgotten.

Sighing, Laine finished the last of the tea and rose reluctantly from the table, aware that the rest of the day stretched endlessly in front of her, and that the prospect of returning to the solitude of the flat held no appeal whatsoever.

She didn't want to be within eyeshot of that empty bedroom. Didn't want to start thinking about Daniel again, wondering where he'd been last night, and who he'd been with. Although she knew that was pretty much inevitable—wherever she was and however hard she might try to avoid it. The same questions had dogged her now for two years, and she was totally and miserably at a loss to know how to clear them from her mind.

Maybe deep hypnosis would help? she reflected wryly. Or even a full frontal lobotomy. Anything that would once and for all remove the images that came back so relentlessly to torment her. The latest, of course, being the imprint of Daniel without his clothes that was now permanently etched into her brain.

Oh, God, how I needed that, she thought with irony.

Perhaps a walk would help? she decided, gingerly testing her ankle. A brief visit to some of her favourite haunts might re-establish the fact that she was back in London. Make her feel more grounded.

Not that she'd ever really wanted to live in the city, but after the end of her marriage her options had been limited, particularly as there had been no Abbotsbrook to return to. Her entire life had had to change, right there and then.

So, as the Beaumonts had decided to give up their tenancy of the Mannion Place flat in favour of a retirement apartment on a golf course complex in Portugal, it had seemed the obvious—the only—answer to move in there with Jamie. Especially when a job as an assistant in a fashionable West End art gallery had been frankly wangled for her by Celia's father, who had some financial interest in the place.

Which meant, on the face of it, she had everything she could possibly ask for, as she consistently and monotonously reminded herself, while she tried desperately to pretend at the same time that there was no great black hole of loneliness and misery at the centre of her little universe.

But she couldn't pretend any more. Nor could she tell herself that Daniel belonged in the past, when here he was—right at the centre of the present.

And neither could she run away again, no matter what the provocation might be.

This time she would stay and face the pain.

It was early evening when she got back to the flat, to discover Daniel was there before her, his briefcase tossed onto one of the sofas and his door firmly closed.

After a brief hesitation, she walked across to his room, and knocked. There was a much longer pause, then the door was flung open and he confronted her unsmilingly, tying the belt of a dark blue silk robe around him.

'Do you have some in-built radar that lets you know when I've just come out of the shower?' he asked caustically.

'I'm sorry.' She wished to heaven she didn't sound so flustered. Or that she didn't remember the last occasion quite so clearly. Although this time he was at least wearing a covering of sorts, she told herself, furious to find that she was blushing. 'I—I need to speak to you, but later will do.'

'Say what you have to say now,' Daniel directed crisply. 'I'm going out later.'

And staying out all night again? The question was bitten back before she was betrayed into asking it aloud.

It seemed infinitely safer to look down at the floor instead, she thought, aware of the flurry of her pulses. 'Actually—I have a favour to ask.'

'Have you, indeed?' In spite of everything, she was aware that he was looking her over sardonically, taking in the primly buttoned blouse and the discreet length of her black skirt. 'Shouldn't you be dressed rather more seductively, in that case? Or have I mistaken the kind of favour?' He paused. 'But then it would hardly be the first mistake I've made where you're concerned—would it, sweetheart?'

'Dan—please.' She took a deep breath, still avoiding his gaze.

'Can we not...? I mean—you—you're not making this very easy for me.'

'Easy—for you?' His laugh was brief and harsh. 'Is that supposed to be a consideration here? Do you think it was *easy* for me to go to my lawyers and tell them I'd been rejected by my bride after less than twenty-four hours of marriage?'

Laine heard the corrosively angry note in his voice, and flinched.

'No,' she said, swallowing. 'No, I don't think that. And I realise, of course, that I have no right to ask for your help, and I apologise.'

'Wait,' he said, as she turned away. 'What is it you wanted?'

She lifted her chin. 'I found a job today, but it involves working in people's homes when they're not there, so I need a character reference.'

He was frowning. 'What kind of a job?'

'With a company called Citi-Clean,' she said, bracing herself. 'They provide daily maid services to blocks of private flats.'

'My God,' he said softly. 'The wheel comes full circle.'

It was the reaction she'd expected, and she accepted it without wincing. 'But at least this time I'll be paid the market rate,' she said. 'I even get a uniform.' She paused. 'But I do need a recommendation. Actually, I need two, but Fiona at the gallery where I used to work is supplying the other. I think she was just thankful I wasn't there to ask for my old job back.' She realised she was babbling and stopped, adding only, 'So—could you?'

'And what am I supposed to say?' Dan asked softly. 'To swear that you're entirely to be trusted and give complete satisfaction at all times? But then I'd be committing a kind of perjury— wouldn't I, darling?'

'If that's how it seems.' Pain lashed out at her, but she forced herself to stand her ground. To speak steadily even though her face was warming helplessly again under his jibe. 'But I think the company's main concern is thieving, and you can't say I've ever stolen anything from you. Maybe you could simply mention that? Give things a more positive spin, perhaps?'

'Perhaps,' he said. 'For a moment there I wondered if you were expecting me to play the knight in shining armour again, and come to your rescue. Because that would be absurdly optimistic, even for you.'

She was turning to go, but she spun round to face him, her eyes blazing. 'Let's get something straight, shall we?' she said, her voice husky. 'Dispel this damned myth once and for all. I am not Elaine, the Lily Maid of Astolat, and I never thought of you as Sir bloody Lancelot—not even for a moment.'

'I'm relieved to hear it,' he said coolly. 'According to the poem he was more than twice her age.' He allowed her to assimilate that for a moment, then added, 'But I'm still capable of the occasional act of chivalry, so leave the address of this cleaning company where I can see it, and I'll get my secretary to write to them.'

She bit her lip. 'I—I'm very grateful.'

'Thanks for the assurance,' he said. 'But I already know the limits you impose on your gratitude, along with all your other warmer emotions. So let's leave this favour as the first and last—shall we, my sweet?'

And he stepped back into the room and closed the door, leaving her standing outside, staring at the closed panels, her arms folded almost protectively across her body.

As if, she thought with bitter self-mockery, she was still attempting some useless defence against a threat that clearly no longer existed. If indeed it ever had.

But as she went slowly back to her own room she found herself remembering that note of anger in his voice. Anger, she realised, mixed with something else much less easy to define. And she shivered.

CHAPTER SIX

THE wheel comes full circle...

Daniel's words seemed to echo and re-echo in her mind as she lay on the bed staring up at the ceiling. And, as she reminded herself, she could hardly defend her decision, or deny its irony. Not to him, at any rate.

She wondered if he too was thinking of the day two years ago when, ten weeks after Si's funeral, he'd walked into the drawing room at Abbotsbrook and found her standing on a rickety pair of steps, struggling to hang the new curtains that had arrived that morning.

'What the hell are you doing up there?'

She hadn't heard him enter the house, let alone the room, and the furious demand from behind her made her jump, and sent the steps into a further paroxysm of wobbles as a result.

'Come down.' The peremptory note brooked no argument, so he didn't actually need to grasp her round the waist with strong hands and lift her bodily from the steps. Yet that was what he did, setting her down to face him, flushed and breathless.

'Dan?' She allowed herself to sound surprised, but braked hard on the instinctive overwhelming delight of seeing him again after all these endless weeks. Of noting almost wistfully how gorgeous he looked. The way the white shirt with the turned-back sleeves emphasised his tan, how the casual charcoal pants enhanced his lean hips and the length of his legs. How that random strand of dark hair always seemed to fall over his forehead, making her always long to smooth it back. Which was impossible.

And then she realised the danger of standing, gaping at him like this. Felt self-conscious too, in her working gear of ancient cut-offs and faded T-shirt, not to mention hot and grubby because she'd just washed down the high window frames.

And hurried into speech. 'My—my mother never mentioned you were expected. Are you staying with us? Because I'll need to see about your room—'

'Your mother has no idea I'm here.' He cut across her incisively. 'I'm staying at a hotel a few miles away, and I've come, having failed to find you at Randalls. What's going on, Laine?'

She shrugged, standing with yards of brocade trailing awkwardly over her arm. 'I left. Didn't Mrs Hallam tell you?'

'Indeed she did, and at some length too,' he said grimly. 'What she couldn't say was why?'

'Because we no longer have a housekeeper, and I'm more use at home.' She spoke with deliberate brightness. 'At least I may be one day. I'm still struggling a bit at the moment.'

There was a silence, then Dan said softly, 'My God, this is unbelievable. What happened to Mrs Evershott?'

'She—left too. We couldn't really afford her any more.'

'So you're doing her job instead?' There was an odd note in his voice. 'At the same salary, I presume?'

'Heavens, no. That's all part of the economy drive.' She forced a smile. 'Although I do get paid, of course.'

'I can imagine. And just how long does your mother intend this situation to continue?'

'Until Abbotsbrook is sold. It went officially on the market yesterday, so who knows?' She held up the brocade. 'Mother's trying to make it seem less shabby to impress the potential buyers when they start flocking in, but I doubt whether a few yards of material will fool them.'

'I don't think so either,' he said dryly. 'And just when did she reach this momentous decision?'

'As soon as I turned eighteen and the terms of the trust no longer applied—oh—and thank you for my gorgeous earrings and the flowers,' she added hurriedly. 'I was going to write, but I wasn't sure where you'd be…'

'Forget about it.' His dark brows were drawn together in a cold frown. 'So, where is your mother? I'd like a word with her.'

'She's at the golf club,' Laine told him. 'But she'll be back around five, and she'll expect to find these curtains up at the windows.'

'Then she can attend to them herself.' Dan took the heavy folds from her and flung them over the back of a chair. 'Risk her own damned neck.'

'But you don't understand,' she protested. 'It's part of my job…'

He said gently. 'You're wrong, Laine. I understand perfectly—apart from asking myself what on earth she's doing at the golf club.'

'She goes there nearly every day,' Laine said, her voice subdued. 'She started having lessons over a year ago, when the new professional first came. His name's Jeff Tanfield.' She paused. 'He's quite a bit younger than she is.'

There was a silence, then Dan said thoughtfully, 'I could do with some strong coffee. Let's go and make it.'

When they were sitting opposite each other at the big scrubbed kitchen table, steaming mugs in front of them, he said, 'So what's really going on, Laine? And I want to know all of it.'

'We're going to live in Andalucia.' Laine struggled to keep her voice from deteriorating into a little wail of desperation. 'At one of those holiday complexes built round a golf course.'

'You as well?'

She nodded. 'When Abbotsbrook is sold Mother's going to invest in the Spanish place, buy into the consortium that owns it. Jeff will go on teaching golf, and Mother will do the administration—look after the guest bungalows. And I'm going to be her assistant.'

'When did you discover this?'

'A few days after my birthday.' She shrugged. Tried to smile. 'I was just—told.'

'I see.' He stirred some cream into his coffee. 'And you agreed?'

She bit her lip. 'I didn't seem to have many other career options open.'

'Tell me,' Dan said, 'is your mother planning to marry this Tanfield?'

'I don't know. Although I heard her having a row with Simon just before he left, and I'm almost sure I heard Jeff's name mentioned. I didn't mean to listen,' she added hastily. 'But she was rather talking at the top of her voice.'

'Then Simon—knew?' he said slowly. 'Well, that makes sense.' He paused. 'What's the age difference between them?'

'Seven—maybe eight years. I'm not too sure.'

He gave her an enigmatic look. 'And you feel that's an insuperable bar to marriage?'

She sipped her coffee, burning her tongue. 'Well, it's usually the other way round—isn't it? The man's generally older than the woman.'

'It can certainly happen,' Dan agreed gravely. 'So, what do you think of your potential stepfather?'

'I suppose he's—all right,' she said slowly, trying to be fair. Then, in a burst of honesty, 'I try not to think about him much at all. Or any of it, for that matter.' She swallowed. 'When Simon was killed I thought things couldn't get any worse, but they have—they have. Everything's suddenly—falling apart, and I don't know how to stop it.'

There was a silence, broken by the sound of an approaching car.

'Your mother?' Dan asked tersely.

She sighed. 'No, that's the station taxi. It will be Candida, arriving for the weekend.'

His brows lifted. 'You surprise me,' he said slowly. 'Does she do a lot of this?'

She nodded. 'She's supposed to be going through Simon's

things,' she said tonelessly. 'Sorting them for charity because Mother doesn't feel up to it yet. But she doesn't seem to have got very far.'

She got up. 'I'd better put the oven on. I made a casserole yesterday, and it just needs heating up.' She paused. 'There's plenty—if you'd like to stay too?'

'No,' he said. 'I don't think so. I have a much better plan. Why don't I take you out to dinner instead?'

Her lips parted in astonishment. 'But I can't. I have to get the rest of supper—the vegetables—a pudding.'

Dan finished his coffee and rose too. 'On the contrary, my sweet, it will do them good to forage for themselves.' He added crisply, 'And I won't take no for an answer, Laine.'

The kitchen door was flung open and Candida swept in, looking disgruntled. 'That train service is a nightmare. I deliberately came early, but it was still crowded with the most ghastly—'

She saw Daniel and halted, her face clearing magically into a ravishing smile. 'Dan—darling. How wonderful. I had no idea you'd be here.'

'And I was just thinking the same about you,' he returned silkily. 'How are you, Candy?'

'Oh—still soldiering on.' She gestured vaguely. 'You know how it is. I come down most weekends to be with poor Angela.' She paused, and sighed. 'We try to be—there for each other.'

'Then I'm surprised you haven't headed straight for the golf club,' Daniel commented blandly. 'I gather that's her chosen refuge these days. But it's good you've arrived early,' he went on, 'because I expect she'll be tired and hungry after a hard afternoon on the fairway, and you can start supper for both of you. Laine and I are going out for dinner.'

'Oh,' Candida said, and her glance flickered between them. Then she smiled again with renewed radiance. 'But that's a terrific idea. Why don't we all go out—make it a real reunion?'

He said, quite gently, 'Because I've invited Laine on her own. It's recompense for missing her birthday.'

'But I'm sure she won't mind.' There was a faintly metallic edge to her voice. 'After all, you were very generous at the time, if memory serves. You mustn't spoil the child too much.'

'I won't,' he said. 'Besides, the recompense is for me—not for her.' He walked round the table, drew Laine to him, and dropped a light kiss on her hair. He said softly, 'Go and make yourself beautiful for me, sweetheart. I'll be back at seven.'

Laine, aware that she was shaking inside, suddenly and uncontrollably, glanced across at Candida, and the two spots of colour now blazing in her cheeks, and decided to make a run for it while her legs would still support her.

And as she flew upstairs to her room she found she was repeating the words 'back at seven' over and over again under her breath, as if they were a good luck charm.

And perhaps I truly thought they were, Laine thought listlessly, recalling how she'd gone through every item in her inadequate wardrobe, trying to find something that would do the occasion justice. At the same time reminding herself with every breath that this was not—*not*—a date. That he was simply being kind.

I knew it then, she thought sadly. Why couldn't I remember it later—when it really mattered?

She heard the flat door bang, and realised that he'd left for the evening, that she was on her own again. Which meant that she could leave her room and move around freely, if she wanted, without the risk of any unwanted encounters.

Except that it just seemed easier to stay where she was as her mind dived back into the deep waters of the past, to that night when her life had changed so completely and so wonderfully— or so she'd thought then.

In the end, she'd decided to wear her summer best of a turquoise wrap-around skirt and white scoop-necked top. Not glamorous or sophisticated, she'd thought wistfully, but the earrings he'd given her would make the outfit a little more special. At the last minute she had added a moonstone pendant on a slender gold chain which had been her seventeenth birthday present from him, watching how it seemed to slide naturally into the faint cleavage between her small breasts and nestle there.

Wondering if he would notice that too, and halting right there, knowing that she was straying into the realms of dangerous fantasy. Reminding herself that the pendant had got her into enough trouble already when, on her birthday evening, she'd gone running into his arms to thank him, seeking his cheek with her lips and somehow finding the warm, lingering pressure of his mouth instead, along with a strange inability to move away, out of range. As she should have done. At once, if not sooner.

An error which, she'd realised, had been lost on no one present— particularly Angela, who'd delivered a stinging rebuke later, telling her she was far too old to fling herself at Daniel like that.

Too old one minute. Too young the next. She'd never known where she stood.

But on that evening, as she'd touched her lips with pale rose colour and recalled the sensation of his mouth on hers, she had felt all too young. And flustered. Thinking, for no fathomable reason, of the clean but so elderly bra and briefs she was wearing. Glad that it wasn't a real date, so there was no chance that they'd ever—that he'd want to—that she'd be expected to…

At which juncture she had told herself sternly to stop thinking, because it was clearly turning her into an idiot, collected her bag and, breathing deeply, gone downstairs.

Angela still hadn't returned, and Candida had been in the drawing room, turning over the pages of a magazine in a way that suggested she'd rather be tearing them to shreds and throwing them at someone.

She'd given Laine a hard stare. 'You're actually planning to wear that—for dinner with Daniel Flynn?'

'My crinoline's at the menders.' Laine pretended to check the contents of her bag, feeling her fragile confidence shredding.

She was rescued almost at once by the shrill of the doorbell and the need to answer it.

'Oh,' she said, almost blankly, finding Daniel waiting on the doorstep, immaculate in a dark suit and a tie the colour of rubies. 'It's you.'

'How many other men are you seeing tonight?'

'But you never ring,' she protested. 'You usually just walk in.'

He glanced past her, his mouth twisting faintly. 'Not when I'm hoping for a fast getaway,' he said, and took her hand. 'Let's go.'

The car was long, low and sleek, and Laine sank down into the soft seat, stifling a sigh of pleasure as she breathed in the expensive smell of leather.

'Is this new?' she asked as the engine purred into life.

'It's always the same car,' he admitted. 'I simply update the model.' He paused. 'Are you learning to drive?'

'No,' she said. 'Not yet.' And probably not at all, she added silently. Not when driving lessons were so expensive. She couldn't visualise her mother footing such a bill—or ever allowing her the use of the household's only car.

She glanced sideways at him. 'You look—well,' she volunteered shyly. 'Very tanned. I thought it was winter in Australia.'

'It is, but I stopped off in America on the way back. Some friends have a house on Cape Cod, and I spent a couple of weeks there.'

'I expect it's very beautiful.'

'Incredibly. Lots of beaches to walk on while you think.'

He seemed to want to think now as well, she reflected rather wistfully as he relapsed into silence, or maybe he was just concentrating on his driving on these narrow country roads.

Not that it really mattered. It was enough just to sit beside him and let her mind flicker through a series of small, impossible dreams.

But when at last he turned the car through a pair of imposing wrought-iron gates she sat up swiftly, her enjoyable reverie over. 'But this is Langbow Manor.' She sounded shocked. 'Are we having dinner here?'

'You've got something against the place?' He looked surprised. 'It seemed fine when I checked into my suite earlier.'

'I've never been here before. But isn't it terribly expensive?'

He slanted a grin at her as he slotted the car into a parking space with expert efficiency. 'That's not an objection I usually get when I take a girl to dinner.'

'No, of course not,' she said, flushing. 'I'm sorry.' Candida's words stung her afresh. 'It's just that I'm not really dressed for somewhere quite as grand.'

He walked round and opened the passenger door. 'I shall be the envy of every man in the place,' he told her softly, and her flush deepened.

Comfort closed round her as soon as she crossed the threshold. The room he took her to was like someone's lovely drawing room, with charming chintz-covered sofas, and chairs grouped round small tables, but within a moment a waiter had arrived beside them. 'For *monsieur* a vodka martini? *Certainement.* And, for *mademoiselle* may I recommend a Kir Royale?'

The drinks were there within seconds, accompanied by a dish of tiny, exquisite canapés, bursting in her mouth with all kinds of delicious and subtle flavours.

'I shan't be able to eat a thing later,' she sighed.

He laughed. 'I think you will.'

And he was right. Because, however nervous and excited she might feel, the watercress mousse she was served, followed by lobster mayonnaise, was just too wonderful for her to leave even a scrap—especially when accompanied by the crisp white wine Daniel had chosen, and which the *sommelier* had brought to them with an air of quiet satisfaction.

She found she could even manage the sweet pastry tart filled with tiny strawberries that ended her meal, while Daniel followed his *vichysoisse* and river trout with a tiny pot of something dark, rich and alcoholically chocolate, of which she sampled a taste.

'This is a magical place,' Laine said, looking around her with shining eyes. They had been given a secluded table in the corner of the Manor's famous conservatory, where the massive vine above their heads was already loaded with bunches of small grapes. Because of the evening's warmth the doors stood open to the garden, and subdued lights had begun to edge the scented borders outside as the daylight faded.

She added, more stiltedly, 'I—I'll remember it always.' She tried to smile. 'I don't think Spain is going to be anything like this.'

'I don't suppose so either,' he said. 'So why go?'

She stared down at the linen tablecloth. 'You speak as if I have a choice.'

'Actually, you do,' he said quietly. 'You could stay here in England—with me.'

The world seemed to stop suddenly. She found she was fighting for breath. For the ability to say, in a voice she barely recognised, 'You're offering me a job?'

'Not exactly.' He smiled at her across the steady flame of the little lamp in the centre of the table. 'I'm asking you to be my wife.'

There was a silence, then she said, in a tone that wobbled slightly, 'If that's a joke, it's not a very kind one.'

He reached out and took her hand, stroking her slender fingers. 'Do I make a habit of being unkind?'

Mutely, she shook her head, trying to banish from her mind the memory of that seemingly endless procession of blondes.

'Well, then.' There was another long silence, then he said on a note of faint amusement, 'My sweet, this hesitation on your part is doing my self-esteem no good at all. You see, I thought you liked me.'

'I do.' *I love you—love you. I always have and I always will…*

'But not enough to marry me—is that it?'

She still couldn't look at him. 'I suppose—I've never thought of you as—the marrying kind.'

He said slowly, 'I could say I've been waiting for you to grow up, but I doubt you'd believe me—not when you've watched me sow a whole series of wild oats.' And, as he saw her bite her lip, he added more urgently, 'Is that the problem, darling—my past? Couldn't we agree to bury it, and simply concentrate on the future instead?'

He paused. 'Unless you're determined to marry another virgin? And I really hope that's not true, for all kinds of reasons.'

She felt her face warm involuntarily, and said on a little gasp, 'Oh, no, I—I'm not.' *I just don't know what to say to someone who's made all my wildest, sweetest dreams come true at once.*

'That,' he said, 'is a definite relief.' He studied her for a moment, then said gently, 'I've startled you, haven't I, sweetheart? I didn't intend that. I thought your female intuition would have warned you why I'd whisked you away with me this evening.'

She tried to smile. 'Perhaps I'm not very female.'

'Now, *that* I don't believe.' Quite casually, he turned her hand over and began to trace a gentle circle in its soft palm with the ball of his thumb. It was the lightest of touches, but Laine felt it piercing her, transfixing her with a shaft of desire so swift, so intense and so totally unexpected that she almost cried aloud in amazement. And in overwhelming need.

She was suddenly melting, liquid with a hunger she'd never even guessed could exist. Aware, too, that her nipples were swelling, hardening against their flimsy constraints, and that her every sense was on fire with the consciousness of him, and his proximity to her. Knew, at the same time that she wanted to be even closer. To be joined to him. To be part of him for ever, totally and irrevocably. To be a woman—his woman.

His voice reached her in a quiet murmur of sound. 'Marry me, Laine.'

Her mouth was dry, the breath catching in her throat, but somehow she managed to whisper back, 'Yes.'

And saw him bend his head in brief acknowledgment.

He released her hand, his mouth twisting in faint ruefulness. 'And now,' he said, 'we'd better go and break the news to your mother.'

She wanted to cry childishly, *But I don't want to go yet. You're staying here—you said so—and I want to be alone with you.*

But of course she said nothing of the kind, just smiled and nodded, and tried to conceal the feeling of inner dread that was uncurling deep inside her, praying that it wouldn't be justified.

She was wrong.

'You want to marry Elaine?' Angela stared at Daniel with narrowed eyes. 'This child? But that's quite absurd. I couldn't possibly agree to any such thing.'

Laine stood beside him, her hand in his, wanting to sink through the floor with humiliation. She was aware of Candida sitting bolt upright, her face like a mask carved from stone, and Jeff Tanfield standing gaping by the drinks table, a glass in one hand, a whisky decanter in the other, as his already pink complexion deepened to crimson.

Daniel said quietly, 'I'm not asking your consent, Mrs Sinclair. I don't have to. I'm merely informing you of our intentions as a matter of courtesy. We plan to be married within the next few weeks.'

'But that's quite impossible.' Angela gestured wildly. 'I have this house to sell—a move to Spain to arrange. I couldn't possibly organise a full-dress wedding as well.'

'You won't be asked to,' Daniel said curtly. 'I'll talk to the Vicar myself about a mid-week date, and the guest-list—on my side anyway—will be minimal. We'll hold a small reception here afterwards, and I'll book the caterer and supply the champagne. The only contribution you need make is to help Laine choose something to wear and send the bill to me.'

'You must have lost your mind,' Angela said shortly. 'For one thing the Daniel Flynns of this world simply do not get married at the drop of a hat to some little nobody in an out-of-the-way place like this.'

He gave her a level look. 'Well, naturally I can't speak for the rest of us, but this Daniel Flynn generally pleases himself. And my current intention is to make Laine my wife as quickly and as simply as possible.' He turned to the girl at his side, lifting the hand he was clasping to his lips. 'Which seems to be what she wants too.'

'Yes.' She found a voice from somewhere. 'I do.'

'And what about her mother in all this?' Jeff Tanfield put

down the decanter and moved forward with sudden belligerence. 'Angela was relying on Elaine's active support in this new venture of ours in Spain. We both were—as she well knows. As part of the team she'd gain valuable and exciting work experience—and also the chance to see something of the world.'

Daniel looked at him, his lip curling. 'She'd provide you with a valuable skivvy, certainly. However, I think Laine will find living and travelling with me rather more amusing than the view from some Spanish laundry room. And I guarantee that the pay and conditions will be better too.'

Angela's laugh was metallic. 'Quite a Cinderella story—isn't it? Except I can't really visualise you as Prince Charming, my dear Daniel. I hope, for her sake, that my daughter knows what she's taking on.'

'If not, I'm sure you'll tell her.' His gaze flicked her contemptuously, then he turned and looked down at Laine, his expression softening. 'The cab's waiting, darling, and the driver has another job later. I have to go.' He saw the desperation in her eyes and smiled reassuringly. 'But I'll be over first thing in the morning to take you shopping for a ring.'

Take me with you, she begged silently. Don't leave me here with them. Take me away now—please.

'Elaine has work to do tomorrow.' Angela's voice was inimical. 'Besides, she'll also be needed to show prospective buyers around.'

'Use the estate agent,' Daniel advised with equal coldness. 'That's what you're paying him for. And I'll get on to an agency and hire someone to take over Laine's kitchen duties.' He put his arm round Laine's waist. 'Now, come and say goodnight to me, sweetheart.'

The night was warm, but Laine shivered as she stood with him at the main door. 'That was so horrible.'

'It could have been worse, believe me.' His tone was wry.

'I don't know how.' There was a touch of desolation in her own voice. 'Dan—I could go on doing the housework here. Mother might appreciate it, and I really don't mind.'

'But I do. I want your hands beautifully soft for our honeymoon.' He grinned teasingly as her face warmed, then bent his head and kissed her swiftly and sensuously on the mouth. 'Sweet dreams,' he told her, and went.

Laine couldn't face going back into the drawing room, so she went upstairs to get ready for bed—although she seriously doubted whether sleep would be an option.

She was just about to switch off her lamp when the door opened and her mother came in.

'Well, you're certainly a dark horse. Feed him some sob story, did you?' Her eyes narrowed. 'Or is there another reason for this hasty wedding? He hasn't got you pregnant, by some mischance?'

Laine's face flamed. 'You know that's not true.'

Angela shrugged. 'I can't think of any other reason for him to bother with you. Although I suppose young flesh will always have its appeal—even to a sophisticate like Daniel Flynn. But marriage?' She laughed harshly. 'Never in this world, my dear.'

Laine sat up very straight, her throat so dry it hurt. 'It doesn't occur to you that he might be in love with me?'

'No, frankly, it doesn't. Is that what he's told you?'

'Of course.' Surreptitiously Laine crossed her fingers under the covers. Because she suddenly realised that Dan had never mentioned the word 'love'. Not when he'd proposed. Not in the cab-ride back to Abbotsbrook. Not while they were saying goodnight.

Not once.

And after Angela had finally left, and she was alone, it was a thought that came back to haunt her over and over again throughout the long night.

CHAPTER SEVEN

So, why did I go on with it, as if everything was all right? Laine asked herself wearily. Because our engagement was a pretty muted affair by anyone's standards. Even with my inexperience I could see that.

Not that he'd been there very much, she reminded herself. And when he had come to see her he'd never stayed at the house, but made Langbow Manor his base again. And, though she'd dined with him there, it had always been in the restaurant. He'd never once suggested that they should be alone together in his suite. And she had been too shy to ask. To tell him how desperately she wanted to go into his arms—to belong to him completely.

'So, where's your ardent lover this weekend?' her mother had once asked witheringly. 'Conspicuous by his absence yet again.'

'Wordwide are involved in a takeover bid for a German magazine company,' Laine had said quietly. 'It's—thrown up some problems, and he needs to be there.' She lifted her chin. 'Besides, we have the rest of our lives to be together.'

'If you say so,' Angela had retorted with a shrug, and left Laine to her own devices.

But even when absent Daniel had been as good as his word on other matters. All the arrangements for the wedding had been in place without fuss or argument, and Laine had found that a bank account had been opened for her, containing more money than she could ever envisage spending.

In addition, a Mrs Goodman had been installed as temporary housekeeper, and had listened patiently to Angela's orders and counter-orders, then gone her own briskly efficient way.

And Laine had received a phone call from a local driving school, requesting her to obtain a provisional licence as a course of lessons had been booked for her.

Everything I could have wished for, she thought. *Except one—the most important—the most crucial of all. The knowledge of his true feelings where I was concerned.*

So why didn't I simply face up to the problem—ask him if he loved me?

Well, she told herself, she knew the answer to that. She'd loved him, and wanted him more than anything in the world. And Daniel's own restraint—those brief, gentle kisses and fleeting caresses which aroused but did not satisfy—had only served to intensify her longing to fever-pitch.

It was as well, she thought, that she'd had so much to do, or she might have gone a little crazy. As a result, she had just allowed herself to be carried forward on the non-stop tide of activity, and tried not to think too much.

One of her tasks had been to sort through her books and other personal possessions, and transfer those she wished to keep to Daniel's London flat—something had made the idea of being his wife seem slightly more real. That and the exquisite ruby and diamond cluster that they'd both spotted at the same moment from the myriad brought out for their inspection, smiling at each other and saying in unison, 'That's the one.'

The tangible evidence that he truly was going to marry her, she'd often thought, touching it gently.

She'd tried to be ruthless and only take the things that really mattered into her new life, giving the rest to the local charity shop. Nothing could have stayed where it was, anyway, because Abbotsbrook had been sold, and the buyer wanted vacant possession almost immediately.

'It's going to be a very expensive care home,' she'd told Daniel on one of the occasions when they were dining together. 'Apparently he has a chain of them.'

'You don't approve?'

Laine sighed. 'It's sold, and my mother is pleased, which has to be a good thing. But I think I always hoped that it would go on being a real home—for a family. That there'd be other children growing up there who'd love it as I did.'

He was silent for a moment. 'Are your memories of it really so happy? I didn't realise.'

'Not all,' she said. 'But a great many of them.' *And most of them to do with you, my love—my love…*

She forced a smile. 'Anyway, it's gone, and as far as Mother's concerned it's *hasta la vista*.'

'I hope she got a good price,' Daniel commented caustically. 'She'll need it to afford the upkeep on the glamorous Mr Tanfield's cosmetic dentistry, quite apart from anything else.'

Laine nearly choked on a mouthful of turbot. 'His smile is— dazzling,' she admitted, trying not to giggle. 'But they do seem happy together, I suppose.'

'Heart-warming,' Daniel said dryly. 'And probably temporary. Has she considered drawing up a pre-nuptial agreement?'

Laine looked down at her plate, aware she was flushing. 'No,' she said. 'I don't think so.' *But, by a horrible coincidence, that was the exact advice she gave me last night—and one of the reasons we're barely on speaking terms right now. The other being she's invited Candida to the wedding.*

'And if he dumps you when the novelty wears off—what then?' Angela had demanded. 'He's a very rich man, my dear—a multimillionaire, no less. He can afford to pay for his pleasures.'

'If he dumps me,' Laine had replied, wincing at the crudity, 'then no amount of money could ever make things better, believe me.'

What neither she nor her mother had foreseen, of course, was that she would be the one who walked away.

It rained on her wedding morning, but the skies brightened

just before she set off to the church, and Celia, who was helping her get ready, told her it was a good omen—the best.

'Do you know where you're going on honeymoon?' she asked. 'Or is it a surprise?'

'We can't go too far away while this takeover business is still simmering.' Laine examined herself from all angles in the mirror, making sure the expensively demure white satin suit she'd chosen hadn't developed any unsightly wrinkles or bulges overnight. 'So Daniel's rented us some secluded hideaway in the depths of the countryside.'

'Good God,' Celia said blankly. 'Does it have plumbing?'

Laine laughed. 'I think so—plus a swimming pool, so it can't be too primitive.' *Although a shed in someone's garden would do, as long as I was with him....*

'And when things settle down at Wordwide he says he'll take me somewhere glamorous and romantic to make up for it,' she added.

'He hasn't a brother, by any chance?' Celia's eyes were dancing. 'Or even a cousin by marriage?'

'Sorry, love.' Laine grinned back at her. 'But I gather the best man's unattached—just.'

Celia gave an exaggerated sigh. 'Then I'll simply have to lower my sights.' She wandered across to Laine's suitcase, open on the bed, and ran a reverent hand over the folds of the delicate white voile nightgown lying on top.

'Wow,' she said. 'Gorgeous, but a total waste of money.'

Laine concentrated fiercely on transferring her engagement ring to her other hand. 'Oh, I thought I'd better have one—in case of fire.'

There was a silence, then Celia said, very gently, 'Lainie—there's nothing to worry about, truly.'

Laine looked at her, stricken. 'Oh, God, is it so obvious?'

'And if it is—so what?' Celia returned robustly. 'You bypass the frogs and get to kiss your prince first time around, that's all.' She paused. 'Although, to be honest, I find it hard to figure how the pair of you have managed to keep your hands off each other.'

Laine's smile didn't reach her eyes. 'Sometimes I wonder too.'

She picked up her bouquet of white roses and freesias and walked to the door. 'It's time we were going.'

Jamie was waiting for her in the hall. 'Hey, you look pretty good,' he informed her with brotherly candour. 'The Lily Maid personified. Maybe Dan isn't completely off his head after all.'

Laine gasped. 'What the hell do you mean by that?'

'Just that he's never seemed the marrying type,' Jamie retorted as he helped her into the back of the waiting car. 'And I bet the news went down like a lead balloon with Ma, although she couldn't really have thought—' He broke off abruptly, then started on a different tack. 'Did you know she insisted we invite that Tanfield bloke to Dan's stag night? Guy, the best man, reckons the slimy git wears a toupée, and if we'd had a bit more to drink we might have found out,' he added, grinning. 'But it turned out to be a pretty sober affair in the end. I guess my future brother-in-law didn't want a serious hangover affecting his bridal performance.'

'It would have to be more than serious to last for twenty-four hours.' Laine spoke lightly, trying to hide her embarrassment.

Jamie gave her a derisive look. 'If he intends to wait that long. There's no law saying sex can only take place under cover of darkness, sister dear. As you may well find out before too long.'

Laine said quietly, 'Could we change the subject, please?'

'Absolutely,' he agreed, unabashed. 'Because it so happens I want a quiet word with you about a business matter.'

She gasped. 'On the way to church?'

'Why not? It's good news, Lainie. The Beaumonts have decided to retire to Portugal—and they've given notice on the flat. It'll be empty by the end of the month, and I'd like to move in there, but as it belongs to you too I have to get your written consent.'

He gave her an anxious look. 'You won't make waves, will you? After all, it's not as if you'll ever need the place yourself.'

'No,' she said. 'I won't. And it's fine with me. Send me whatever I need to sign when I come back from honeymoon.'

There were more people at the service than she'd expected, and not all of them wishing her well, she thought with a pang as she stood beside Daniel at the altar. But the ceremony itself, with its calm traditional words, was a comfort and a reassurance. She heard Daniel promise to love her until death, and vowed she would do the same. And the warmth of his mouth on hers became a benediction that made her tremble inside.

As they sat together in the back of the car returning them to Abbotsbrook for the brief reception, Daniel drew her close against him, his lips caressing her hair. He said softly, a smile in his voice, 'Well, Mrs Flynn. Here we are at last.'

And Laine, staring down at her wedding ring, felt joy unfurl inside her like the buds on a springtime tree.

As soon as the toasts had been drunk and the cake cut, she slipped away to change. Celia, she saw with amusement, was flirting with the best man, and clearly did not wish to be disturbed.

But, Laine thought, I'd rather be on my own too—for these last moments in my old home before I leave it for ever as Dan's wife.

She was in bra and briefs, just stepping into the pale yellow shift she planned to wear for the journey, when there was a knock on the door.

Daniel, she thought, her heart leaping, and called, 'Come in.'

But when she saw her visitor she felt sick with disappointment.

'Candida,' she said. 'What a surprise.'

'It's been a pretty surprising day all round,' the older girl returned. She walked across the room, and sat down without invitation, on the edge of the bed, next to the case which, thankfully, Laine had just closed. 'So Daniel actually went through with it. I'm amazed.'

Laine drew up her dress, sliding her arms into the brief cap sleeves, then began to fasten the long line of small fabric-covered buttons which closed its front.

She said quietly, 'If you've come here to be unpleasant, I'd prefer you to leave.'

'Oh, very dignified,' Candida said mockingly. 'The publishing tycoon's lady to the life. He may not want to be married to you, but at least you'll play the part—while it lasts.'

Laine walked to the door and opened it. 'That's quite enough,' she said stonily. 'Now, get out.'

'When I'm good and ready. And only when I've finished saying what I came to say. So I suggest you come back and listen. I really do.

'That's better,' she went on, as the younger girl slowly closed the door and went over to sit on her dressing stool. 'You see, Elaine, I actually feel sorry for you. When Daniel said "I will" today, you must have thought you'd just won the major prize in life's lottery.'

She smiled slowly. 'But what you really heard, my poor child, was a man reluctantly stepping into the shoes of his dead friend. Steeling himself to accept responsibility for Simon's hopeless and helpless little sister—just as he once promised.

'A promise he made totally against his will, because he never believed he'd be called on to keep it. Because he was counting on Simon coming back and letting him off the hook.

'Only Simon didn't come back. Not for him—or anyone.' Her voice took on a vicious note. 'And suddenly Dan had you—round his neck like an albatross—weeping and wailing about the hand life had dealt you, with no qualifications and no prospects. Making him pity you all over again, and reminding him that he'd given his word he'd look after you.'

Laine said thickly, 'I—don't believe you.'

'Of course not.' Candida shrugged lightly. 'And I don't blame you. In your shoes I'd much rather persuade myself that Daniel had fallen in love with me. Except that his attentions haven't been exactly marked since your engagement—or before it, for that matter.'

She gave a silvery laugh. 'In fact I'd be most surprised to discover that you're any more than just good friends. Although I'm sure Daniel will do his duty by you tonight.'

'Duty?' Laine lifted her chin disdainfully, trying to conceal the fact that her heart was thudding like a battering ram against her ribcage, and that she felt sick to her stomach with fright. 'You imagine that's all it will be?'

Candida regarded her calmly. 'You still don't believe me, do you? Would you like proof?'

No, thought Laine. I want you to disappear. I want the last five minutes never to have happened. I want the door to open all over again, and Daniel to come in and take me in his arms.

She sat and watched as Candida unfastened the clasp on her slim black bag and extracted a folded sheet of notepaper.

'I'm afraid I found this among Simon's things,' she said. 'Please believe it gives me no pleasure to show it to you.'

'Then why are you doing so?' Laine was thankful to see that her hand didn't tremble as she took it.

'Because you stand in grave danger of making a fool of yourself, and seriously embarrassing Daniel as well, and I'm sure you don't want that. So it's obviously preferable that you understand the terms of your marriage from the outset, and don't ask for more than he can give.'

As soon as she unfolded the sheet Laine recognised Daniel's handwriting. The letter began abruptly.

Si—I apologise about last night. I know we both said things we now regret. But being suddenly asked to accept responsibility for Laine's welfare if you don't make it back from Annapurna frankly knocked me sideways. As I told you, I don't want that kind of involvement. Not any more. You know my reasons for this, and I'm sorry you objected to them, because they are not ever going to change.

However, I've thought things over since, and I concede you have valid reasons for being concerned about Laine, especially if you're going to be absent for any length of time. Therefore, in spite of my personal reservations, I accept the obligation to take charge of her in your place, even though it's a hellish burden as things are. But I realise there is probably no one else you can ask.

One more thing. Simon, man, this Annapurna trip sounds like really bad news. You clearly feel it, and I'm certain of it. I'm also sure it can't be too late to back out, even now.

But, at the same time, I know that's not your style, so all I can say is if you go, make bloody certain you come back safely, or you could wreck my life and Laine's, as well as destroying your own. Just don't do this to us all. Please. As ever, Dan.

Laine read it through, then read it again more slowly, until every line, every word, every syllable was etched into her aching brain. Never to be forgotten—or forgiven.

She raised her head and looked at the smiling face of the woman lounging on her bed, and she wanted to claw at that smile until the blood ran.

Instead she said, with a soft dignity she hadn't known she possessed, 'Thank you. Do—do you want it back?'

'I don't think so. It's served its purpose, so you keep it.' Candida uncoiled herself, rose, and walked to the door. 'Poor Elaine,' she said. 'I've shattered your illusions, haven't I? But surely that's better coming from me than from Dan?

'Besides, you've married the man you're crazy about—and half a loaf is always preferable to no bread at all, or so they tell me. Just keep reminding yourself of that, and I'm sure everything will be fine.'

The door closed softly, and she was gone.

When she could move, Laine stood up and went across to her case. She opened it, slipped the folded letter into one of the side pockets, and zipped it away.

As if by hiding it she could somehow erase the memory of it too—of the stinging phrases that had brought her life crashing around her.

'Hellish burden,' she said aloud, trying the words on her tongue as she looked at herself in the mirror. Saw the ghost in the half-buttoned dress, with eyes like bottomless pits.

And thought, Oh God, what am I going to do? *What can I do?*

She had still found no answers to those questions some two hours later, when she arrived with Daniel at their honeymoon destination.

It was as if she'd become two people, she thought as she sat beside him in the car, looking at the flying countryside with unseeing eyes. One who smiled with the expected radiance of a new bride, who chatted and kissed people goodbye, then tossed her bouquet so that Celia caught it. And another secret person who waited numbly in some inner darkness and prayed for the pain to cease.

She could not remain in the marriage. That was one certainty to emerge from her silent soul searching. The other, more importantly, was that Daniel must never find out that she knew why he'd married her—must never realise that she'd seen that wretched letter, and the agonising truth it contained. That, at eighteen years old, her marriage was a myth and she herself simply an unwanted wife. An obligation and a responsibility that he'd been forced to acquire.

But, although she might know his secret, he could not be allowed to know hers, or she would die of humiliation.

Oh, why did I let him see that I dreaded going to Spain? she asked herself desperately. I should have pretended that it was an adventure— an ideal opportunity for me—and by doing so released him from the coercion of his promise to Simon.

'You're very quiet,' Daniel observed suddenly, startling her from her confused and unhappy thoughts. 'You've hardly said two words since we set off. Are you all right?'

'I'm fine.' *When had she learned to be such an accomplished liar?* 'A little tired, maybe, after all the rushing about of the past few weeks, that's all.'

'I should have been around more.' He was frowning slightly, his swift sideways glance at her concerned. 'I let that damned takeover occupy too much of my time. But all that stops right here,' he added softly. 'From now on, I intend to concentrate solely on you, my sweet.'

Don't call me that, she thought. Don't look at me as if I matter. Above all—don't be kind—because I can't bear it. Not when I know that's all there is…

'I hope you like the cottage,' he went on. 'A couple called Jackson run the place for the owners—do all the cooking and cleaning, and look after the garden.

'It sounds wonderful.' A mechanical response, as if she'd been programmed.

And of course it *was* wonderful—'cottage' being a total misnomer for the charming redbrick house rambling round three sides of a courtyard. The Jacksons, large, placid and clearly discreet, were waiting to welcome them, and to take their bags up to a large bedroom overlooking the rear garden.

The window was open, and Laine went straight to it, trying not to look as if she was deliberately ignoring the wide bed with its pretty patchwork coverlet and snowy linen. She knelt on the cushioned window seat, inhaling the scent of the flowers drifting up from below and touching with her fingertips the petals of the Gloire de Dijon rose that covered the adjacent wall.

'Happy?' Daniel spoke from behind her, his voice gentle.

'Of course,' she returned. 'It's beautiful.' She turned, glancing round her. 'Although there doesn't seem to be a lot of cupboard space.'

'My God,' he said. 'How much stuff have you brought?' He waited a moment for her to respond to his teasing smile, but in vain. He added more slowly, 'There's another room across the passage. I can put my things in there, if you want. Give you more space.'

'Thank you,' she said. 'Then perhaps we could have some tea?'

'A delightful idea,' Daniel said cordially. 'And when, if ever, am I going to be allowed to kiss you? Let alone undo the buttons on that intriguing dress?'

She remembered Jamie's casual comment. Thought how, only a few hours before. she would have gone with shy eagerness into his arms, yielding her mouth and her body to his possession.

Now, she managed a nervous laugh. 'Daniel—it's broad daylight—the middle of the afternoon.'

'As you wish,' he said, after a pause. 'After all, I've waited so long already that a few more hours won't kill me.' He moved away towards the door. 'I'll speak to Mrs Jackson about your tea, then go and unpack.'

Alone, Laine found she was staring at the bed as if hypnotised. The bed where Daniel would later perform his duties as her husband, with probable skill and enjoyment. Because he was a man, and she was new and available. And, as she'd learned from Celia and other more worldly-wise friends, where men were concerned sex and love were not necessarily part of the same equation.

For Daniel, she thought, it would be little more than a conditioned reflex, and she shivered.

I can't let him touch me, and I can't touch him... Otherwise I'll be lost for ever—his creature, existing on whatever kindness he chooses to show me. Having to make believe that we have a real marriage, a union of minds as well as bodies.

She unpacked and put away her things, leaving the letter in its hiding place. She didn't need to look at it again. Every bit of it was seared into her memory.

Downstairs, she drank her tea in the drawing room, and pretended to eat a scone, while Daniel, not pretending at all, read the financial pages of the daily paper with narrow-eyed attention.

Afterwards she went for a walk in the garden, Daniel having declined her stilted invitation to accompany her with equal politeness, and realised she was deliberately prolonging her stroll, lingering over every plant as if she was memorising it for an examination.

She also discovered the swimming pool, totally secluded in a high-walled garden, where espaliered fruit trees spread their branches over the elderly red brick. It was a warm and sheltered place, the sun still high enough to make a swim seem enticing, and for a moment she wistfully considered going back to the house and changing into her bikini.

It occurred to her, too, that if this was a real honeymoon, and

Dan and she had found the pool together, he would have dealt swiftly with the buttons on her dress, laughing away her protests, and swimming costumes would have become entirely superfluous for them both. She turned away, stifling a sigh.

'Mrs Jackson suggests dinner at eight,' Daniel said when she got back to the house. 'Does that fit in with your plans?'

She looked at him, startled. 'I—I have no plans.'

'No?' There was faint irony in his voice. 'My mistake.'

She hesitated. 'Do we—dress for dinner?'

His brows lifted. 'Isn't that a little formal—for just the two of us?'

'Yes, of course. I—I wasn't thinking.'

He sent her an enigmatic look. 'How I wish that were true,' he said, and returned to the newspaper, and the crossword he was completing.

Laine was hungry, but she had to force herself to eat the delicious food Mrs Jackson provided—smoked trout, followed by lamb cutlets with new potatoes and tiny broad beans, with a creamy mousse made from fresh strawberries for dessert.

The meal was conducted mainly in silence, although Laine made an effort to speak whenever the Jacksons were in the room. But it was making conversation, she realised, rather than talking, and to judge by his sardonic expression Dan knew it too.

Coffee was served in the drawing room, but Laine declined the brandy they were offered.

'Would you like to listen to some music?' Dan asked when they were alone again. He nodded towards the shelves that flanked the fireplace. 'There seems to be a fair selection.'

'Thank you.' She put down her empty cup. 'But I'm tired. I think I'll—go up. That is, if you don't mind?'

'Why should I?' He smiled at her. 'The idea has much to recommend it. But I think I'll stay down here for a while. Finish my drink. Listen to a CD, perhaps.' He paused. 'What shall I pick, Laine? A sonata—or a whole symphony?'

She hesitated by the door. 'I don't know. It's your choice.'

'Is it?' He sent her a reflective glance. 'I wonder.'

As she went up the stairs she heard the first sombre chords of Elgar's cello concerto following her. It was a favourite of hers, and she should have been listening to it with him, curled into the curve of his arm, sharing brandy from the same glass. Not going to her room alone.

She went quietly through the rituals of preparation, as if she was a real bride. Took a bath that was warm but not too hot. Rubbed her favourite lotion into her skin and applied a more intense version of its scent to her pulses, her throat and between her breasts. Brushed her hair until it hung to her shoulders like tawny silk. Put on the filmy high-waisted nightgown with its satin ribbon straps.

Then sat on the edge of the bed in the lamplight and waited to end her marriage.

She heard him come upstairs, and the breath caught in her throat, but he went into the other room, and it was twenty minutes before her own door finally opened and they confronted each other, husband and wife, in the shadowy room.

Dan closed the door quietly behind him and leaned back against its panels, looking at her in silence. He was barefoot, clearly wearing nothing but the white towelling robe, and for a moment everything she'd ever felt for him stormed into her consciousness, and she wanted him so badly that her resolve almost faltered. Almost, but not quite.

He said, very softly, 'How incredibly lovely you look.' And took a step towards her.

Immediately she raised a hand in negation, halting him. 'No,' she said. 'No—don't come any closer. Don't come near me.'

'Ah,' he said, and there was a note almost of resignation in his voice.

When he spoke again, his voice was gentle. 'Darling, it's been obvious since we got here that you've been developing a problem about sleeping with me. But I promise you that keeping me at arm's length won't solve a thing.'

'It's not just sleeping with you,' Laine said, the words stumbling over each other. 'It's more—much more than that. It's everything. You see, I've made a terrible—an unforgivable mistake.'

He stared at her. 'What mistake?' he demanded roughly. 'What the hell are you talking about?'

She swallowed. 'Marrying you. I should never have agreed—never have done it. But I was desperate—and then it was all such a rush—I didn't have time to think properly—to consider what I was doing. *You* rushed me,' she added almost wildly.

'But as soon as I was alone with you I realised. It occurred to me for the first time what being on honeymoon with you would mean—and I knew that I couldn't do it. That I couldn't—be your wife. Not ever.

'You asked me once if I liked you enough to marry you, but I don't—I don't. Only I never knew it before, and I'm sorry—I'm so sorry.'

Her voice broke, and she looked away from him. Looked at anything but him. His face, stark with shock in the lamplight.

Listened to the crackle of the silence between them.

Which he broke at last, his voice quiet. 'I hardly think being sorry really covers the situation.' He drew a deep breath. 'Laine, listen to me, darling—please. I was always afraid that it was too soon for this level of intimacy between us. Felt that I should have given you more time—maybe even courted you differently. I hardly know any more.

'But you really don't have to be nervous about sharing a bed with me,' he added huskily. 'I can be patient and I will, I promise you—on all I hold sacred. I'll wait until you're ready to give yourself however long it takes, and I'll be so gentle.'

He took another step towards her. 'But trust me now, sweetheart, and don't turn me away from you tonight. Let me stay—even if it's simply to hold you. I'll be content with that. I swear it. I won't ask for another thing.'

'No.' She got to her feet, trembling. 'No—I can't—I won't.'

He said hoarsely, 'Dear God, Laine, this is our wedding night. Do you want me to go on my knees and beg?'

'No,' she said again, almost violently. 'You're not listening to me. And you have to listen. You must understand that I—I can't bear you to touch me or even be near me. That the thought of letting you do any of the things you'll eventually want fills me with disgust. And that I'd rather die than sleep with you.

'Because it's over—over—do you hear me? I shouldn't be here. Shouldn't have done this dreadful thing.' Her voice rose wildly. 'And you have to let me go. *Let me go.*'

As the words died into silence she watched his face harden in anger and distaste. Heard his voice reach her from some bitter ruined wasteland that she recognised from her own inner despair.

'Don't worry. You're a cheat, a liar and a bitch. And I'll let you go. Because I wouldn't soil my hands on you now if you crawled to me over broken glass.'

Then he was gone, and she sank back on her empty marriage bed, her throat raw, her hands pressed to her burning eyes, too sick and unhappy even to cry.

CHAPTER EIGHT

AND in all that pleading he'd never once said he loved her. She'd thought it then, during all those endless sleepless hours. She remembered it now, two years later.

And wasn't that enough to justify the stand she'd taken? The sheer necessity not to be merely an obligation he'd acquired? To be a 'burden'—that shaming, unendurable word which still had the power to flay the skin from her bones.

No real mention of passion either, she thought objectively. Just endless restraint and consideration, as there'd been throughout their engagement. Surely real desire couldn't be so easily suppressed?

Because there'd been no attempt to change her mind by physical means either. No move to walk across and take her in his arms, whether she wanted it or not. No kissing her into submission before throwing her across the bed and dealing with her wisp of a nightgown in the way she'd originally planned, before he—he…

Before he—*what?*

Pathetically, she still only knew in theory, except that she was unswervingly certain that telling her he adored her and couldn't live without her had to be part of it.

If he'd wanted her at all, she thought, surely he'd have—tried…?

She rolled over on the bed, burying her face in the pillow. Twenty years old, she jeered in self-derision, and still a virgin, a walking anachronism, without any temptation to be otherwise, while the only man she'd ever wanted continued to enjoy his resumption of bachelorhood with a varied selection of willing ladies.

Wasn't that why she'd headed for Florida, hoping that out of sight might eventually mean out of mind? Except that it patently hadn't worked.

She could only hope and pray she wasn't destined to be a one-man woman, unable to make a new life for herself or dispel this nightmare of loneliness and need that had haunted her since that night.

That night. She'd slept at last, somewhere near dawn, if memory served, forced into it by sheer exhaustion of body and spirit.

And had woken to a room full of sunlight and the awareness of someone knocking at the door. Stomach churning with apprehension, Laine had sat up, pulling the covers around her, and called 'Come in.'

Mrs Jackson had entered briskly with a tray. 'Good morning, madam. Your tea. And Mr Flynn asks if you will join him for breakfast at nine-thirty,' she added, her placid face not betraying a glimmer of curiosity about these extraordinary newlyweds.

'Yes,' Laine said numbly. 'Yes, of course.'

She was white-faced and hollow-eyed when she ventured downstairs, dreading his anger, his bitterness.

Instead, he was sitting at the breakfast table, calmly drinking his coffee. He rose politely when he saw her, his face expressionless.

'Good morning.' A cool, formal greeting. 'The toast is fresh, but if you prefer something cooked just ring the bell.'

'Toast is fine.' Her voice was a croak as she sank into the seat opposite.

'Then we shan't be disturbed.' He paused. 'I've given the matter some thought, and I've decided it would be better to stay here for the next two weeks, as arranged.'

'Is that really necessary?' Laine couldn't hide her dismay.

Dan shrugged. 'Anything else would cause the kind of

comment and speculation that neither of us will appreciate,' he countered. 'But we'll continue to live in total separation.'

His mouth curled. 'And you certainly need have no fear that I'll ever enter your bedroom again.' He poured himself some more coffee.

'As for your unfortunate "mistake" in marrying me,' he went on. 'That can be quite easily rectified. Tell your family and friends whatever story you please, but in reality we can have the whole thing discreetly annulled on the grounds of non-consummation. I'll tell my lawyers to contact yours.'

'The slate wiped clean,' she commented huskily.

'As you say.' His smile grazed her skin. 'Meanwhile I'll relieve you of my presence here as much as possible, though we'll have to meet at dinner. We can hardly expect Mrs Jackson to serve us at different times.'

He added, 'This is an attractive part of the world, and I looked forward to doing some sightseeing while we were here. I'll still do so—but alone, naturally. You, darling, will have to amuse yourself as best you can.'

He leaned back in his chair, his gaze insolent. 'Not the idyll I had planned—exploring the countryside by day and each other at night—but, hey, you can't have everything.'

She winced. 'Dan—don't, please.'

'Don't what? Upset you with a passing reference to my former carnal intentions?' His voice had the edge of a scalpel. 'Believe me, my girl, you've got off lightly.'

She lifted her chin. 'Whether I believe you or not, the lock on my bedroom door has no key. I'd like it found.'

'Tough,' he said curtly. 'My room, however, has a lock *and* a key, and last night I used them.'

'You did?' Her eyes widened. 'Why?'

'Because I have a pretty foul temper at times,' he said brutally. 'And for a time there I was seriously tempted to walk back into your room and treat you in a way I'd probably have regretted for the rest of my life.

'But not any more.' He pushed back his chair and stood up. 'And on that thought I'll leave you in whatever peace you feel you deserve.'

Peace, Laine thought, being translated into fourteen days and nights of unalleviated misery—on her part at least.

It was on the last evening that they finally exchanged more than a few words.

'We have to consider what arrangements to make when we go back to London tomorrow,' Dan said, halting her on her way upstairs for one of the early nights that had become her norm. 'Abbotsbrook will be empty by now, and your mother has probably already left for Spain, so I suggest you use my apartment as a temporary base and I'll move out.'

'No,' she said. 'I couldn't live there.' She swallowed, remembering her visit—how she'd visualised their life together. 'Not possible. Besides, I have somewhere to go,' she added quickly. 'Jamie's moving into the flat in Marrion Place, and as half of it's mine I'll join him.'

'Fine.' He shrugged. 'Let me know the exact address, so I can send over your things.' He paused. 'I shall, of course, continue to pay you the same allowance as before we were married, and it will be adjusted upwards after the annulment goes through.' His mouth twisted. 'I wouldn't want you to suffer just because you don't fancy me.'

'And I'll see you in hell before I take a penny of yours,' she flamed at him. 'I want nothing from you. I'll get a job and support myself.'

She took a breath. 'Oh, and before I forget.' She wrenched off her wedding and engagement rings and held them out to him. 'These belong to you.'

'I think not.' He made no attempt to take them. 'So you keep them, my sweet. Otherwise sell them, or throw them away. Whatever. But it's entirely down to you. Because I never want to see them again.'

In the end she been unable to decide on their disposal, so she'd put them in the bank, along with her grandmother's pearls. Where they still remained.

And he'd still offered her the money, in spite of what she'd said. It had been a battle, but in the end he'd been forced to accept no for an answer yet again.

However, admitting her marriage was over had been simpler than she'd believed possible—principally because so few people had known it had taken place. And she'd told no one what had really happened—not even Celia, in whose bewildered company she'd broken down at last, weeping uncontrollably with her head buried in her friend's lap until she had no tears left.

And especially not Jamie, who'd held her totally to blame, and told her frankly she didn't know when she was well off.

'So what went wrong?' he'd demanded. 'Found out, did you, that he'd still got a mistress tucked away somewhere?'

'No,' she'd said, adding with a painful lack of caution, 'Has he?'

'How would I know? Dan keeps his private affairs extremely private. Or he did until recently, anyway. Now he seems to have moved his life into the fast lane for all to see. But he's returned you, unused, to store,' he'd added with a shrug. 'So why should you care, missy?'

Why indeed? Laine thought now, wincing. But I did care—hence Andy, and the whole boiling mess that's resulted.

Of course now that Dan had gone out there was no real reason to hide away in her room any longer. She could sing at the top of her voice, paint her toenails in different colours, and turn cartwheels stark naked if the mood took her. Alternatively, she could finish up last night's chicken and watch television.

Option B, I think, she told herself, pulling a face. Just in case he plans to come back early, or even at all.

But she ended by scraping most of her meal into the wastebin, telling herself that her all-day breakfast had certainly lived up to its name.

She made some coffee and curled up on the sofa, flicking through the movie channels until she found an old black and white romantic drama she'd always loved. But for once the magic didn't work for her, and she was restless, her attention constantly wandering.

You're doing it again, she derided herself. Wondering where he is. Waiting for him to come back. And it has to stop. Because you're wasting your time. He didn't want you then, or not in any way that mattered, and he doesn't want you now.

So perhaps you don't believe in happy endings any more, she added, and switched off the television.

She rinsed out her beaker, made sure the kitchen was immaculate, then went into the living room, tidying things away, and plumping up cushions, as if she was removing all trace of her presence.

We're back in honeymoon territory here, she thought wryly, with Dan doing exactly as he pleases while I—I try not to be noticed. Or to displease him.

My God, we even occupy rooms opposite each other, all over again. At the cottage we were divided by the width of a passage, and now it's the length of a room, but it might as well be from here to the planet Jupiter, because as a space it's still impassable.

And the question I can't seem to avoid is: if I could go back to the day—the night—of our wedding, would I do things any differently? Would I tear up the letter and settle for the half-loaf after all, because I'd rather be miserable with him than without him?

If I'd really become his wife, could I ever have made him love me—treat me as his woman, his equal, instead of Simon's little sister, too young and silly to manage her life? Would he ever have told me his problems, or turned to me needing comfort?

I was so tempted that night to go to him and ask him to forgive me, she thought with a bitter sigh. So tempted that once I even made it halfway across the passage. But I didn't dare knock at his door, and when I heard next morning that he'd locked it I was thankful that I hadn't risked it—because there's only so much humiliation you can take in twenty-four hours.

And now here we are, thrown together again, and no respite available except the oblivion of sleep.

She turned and went slowly into her room. She didn't feel particularly weary, yet once in bed she found herself drifting off almost immediately. At some point she began dreaming that she was back on the boat. That she was in a cabin, with everything movable pushed up against the door, because Andy was outside looking for her and he was angry.

But when the door slowly opened, in spite of her efforts, it was Dirk Clemmens who came in, smiling and licking his lips as he reached for her with those repulsive fat hands covered in ginger hair, and she was being forced to touch him in turn, pushing against his chest to keep him off. But he was too strong, too determined, and Laine threw back her head and began to scream and scream, although she knew there was no one to come to her rescue.

And Dirk Clemmens was telling her to be quiet. Saying that she must wake up and be quiet. But she went on struggling and shouting, swimming up through layers of sleep to open dazed eyes and discover that there was no boat. That she was in her room at the flat, with the lamp lit, and that it wasn't Dirk Clemmens holding her and trying to hush her but Dan, kneeling on the bed beside her.

'You,' she said hoarsely, pulling away from him. 'Oh, God, what are *you* doing here?'

'Trying to stop you screaming the place down,' he said tersely. 'Hopefully before the neighbours call the police and have me arrested for rape and/or murder.' He was wearing the blue silk robe. His hair was dishevelled, and he looked sleepy and bad-tempered in equal amounts.

'I'm sorry,' she muttered, looking away. 'I was having a bad dream.'

'Somehow I'd managed to figure that for myself.' He released her and moved to sit at the edge of the bed, tightening the belt of his robe. 'I hope it's not the recurring sort, or I'll have to buy earplugs.'

'It's not funny.' Her voice cracked in the middle, and she realised with shock that she was close to tears. 'It was horrible, and I was so frightened. I—I thought he'd come to find me.'

'He?' Dan queried. 'Who is he?'

She shuddered convulsively. 'A vile man called Dirk Clemmens. He was just a really loathsome client to begin with, but then Andy sold him the boat, and I somehow became part of the deal—left quite deliberately for him to use, as if I was part of the fixtures and fittings.'

She swallowed. 'That's how I hurt my ankle—getting away from him. I suppose I was still scared subconsciously that he'd trace me—follow me. Still find some way of making me do what he wanted.'

'You were sold to him?' Dan's brows rose. 'I understood slavery had been abolished.'

Her fingers twisted the edge of the sheet. 'Not the sort he had in mind.'

His mouth tightened. 'But didn't you own a share in the boat?' he demanded. 'How could it be sold away from you?'

'I don't know.' She shook her head. 'I don't think my name was properly registered on the paperwork. I should have made sure it was all foolproof, but I didn't, because I wanted to get away from England in a hurry, and Andy was able to walk away with the lot.'

Her eyes blurred suddenly. 'Perhaps Simon was right about me. Maybe I'm not fit to cope on my own.' And stopped, gasping, as she realised what she'd just said. That she'd practically admitted she knew about the deal he'd struck with Simon. The deal that had led inevitably to the sheer disaster of their marriage.

On top of that, it wouldn't be hard for him to work out her pathetic reasons for wanting to leave the country so fast.

Yet, instead of adding two and two, and coming up with the right answer, his mind seemed to be elsewhere.

'But this Andy was your lover,' he said slowly. 'So what went wrong? Had you quarrelled?'

'Not as such,' Laine said evasively. Let him think that Andy and I were involved in every way, she thought. It's safer than the truth—that *he's* the only man I've ever thought of or ever wanted. That there's not been anyone else. Please let him never know that. Because I can't be pitied by him any more. I just can't. It would kill me...

'I think we'd just reached the parting of the ways,' she added slowly, collecting her scattered thoughts. 'But, unfortunately for me, he realised it before I did. I came back to the boat one day and he'd simply—gone, leaving the ghastly Clemmens in his place, waiting for me, armed with Andy's personal recommendation.' She tried to speak brightly, felt the full horror of the dream welling up inside her again, choked, and burst into tears.

Dan said something under his breath, then moved swiftly to lie beside her, taking her shaking body into his arms and stifling her tearing sobs against his shoulder.

'It's all right.' Laine was aware of his voice soothing her, his hand stroking her hair. 'Everything's all right. He's not here, and he never will be. There's nothing to be scared of.'

But it was no longer just the dream, and she knew it. Knew that she was weeping for the wasteland her life had become. For the moment when her dream of happiness had crashed into crippling reality, and for every lonely, bewildered, hopeless hour since.

And she clung to him, her wet face pressed against him as she wept, at the same time breathing the unique scent of his skin through the thin silk of the robe like a starving child reaching for food.

Slowly, imperceptibly, she began to grow calmer, the intensity of the trembling starting to fade, the sobs not as harsh in her aching throat. Realised that her hand was clasping his, their fingers entwined.

She lifted her head, looking up at him through damp and matted lashes. 'I'm sorry,' she murmured, her voice catching. 'I'm so sorry.'

'Don't be.' He took a handful of tissues from the box on the night-table and passed them to her. 'They say that weeping's cathartic.'

'Do they?' Laine began to dry her face, suddenly conscious of how awful she must look. Her nose had almost certainly turned pink, and her hair was sticking in tangles to her tear-stained skin. And the striped cotton nightshirt she was wearing did her no favours either. 'I always wonder who "they" are.'

'Heaven only knows,' he said. 'But let's hope they're right for once.' He sat up, carefully detaching himself. Putting her back against the pillow. 'Now, try and get some sleep.'

She maintained her clasp on his hand. 'I don't want to close my eyes,' she whispered, her mouth trembling. 'Not yet. I know it's stupid, and I'm behaving like a child, but I'm frightened he'll be there, waiting for me.'

'You really think he has that much staying power?' He shook his head. 'Never in this world. You're perfectly safe.'

'Then make me feel safe.' The words seemed to come from nowhere, hoarse, shaken, pleading. 'Stay with me, Dan. Don't leave me. Don't go.'

There was a silence, then he said, in a voice she barely recognised, quiet with bitterness, 'Dear God, Laine, you don't ask much.'

He lay down again on top of the covers, drawing her back to him, holding her close, pillowing her head on his chest.

She sighed, drowsy contentment closing in on her, aware that her eyes were already growing so heavy she could barely keep them open. Knowing at the same time that he was still too far away, when she needed him so much closer, with all barriers between them gone at last.

She said in a small slurred voice, 'Don't you want to…?'

'I want you to sleep,' he said, more gently. 'And not to dream. Now, hush.'

And she sighed, smiling, and slid down into the comfort of the darkness, lulled by the steady rhythm of his heartbeat under her cheek.

She woke early the next morning and stretched languidly, feeling rested and relaxed for the first time since her return.

Then paused as the events of the previous night came rushing back to assail her.

She sat up abruptly, all lingering drowsiness fled. No, she thought, horrified. That can't have happened. I couldn't possibly have wept all over Dan, then begged him to sleep with me. Not even *I* could have done something so utterly stupid. I must have gone from one weird dream into another. That's the only explanation.

It did not, however, explain the wrinkling of the cover beside her, or the significant dent in the adjoining pillow, where, she also realised, she could still detect the scent of his cologne, faint, subtle but quite unmistakable.

Irrefutable evidence that he had indeed spent at least part of the night in her room. But on her bed, not actually *in* it.

Which, of course, is such a comfort, and makes everything just fine. She groaned, pressing her hands against her burning face. Oh, you idiot. You witless, senseless idiot. What in hell did you think you were doing?

And what on earth am I going to say when I next see him? I could try the truth. That for a moment there I forgot everything except the need to be in his arms—a need that he clearly doesn't share. In fact he doesn't even have to pretend that he finds me desirable—not any more.

Maybe I should keep it light and practical. Be rueful about his disturbed night and my all-time emotional low. Promise that if I have any more nightmares I'll stick my head under the pillow.

Another olive branch might not come amiss either, she thought, as she slid out of bed. On the lines of one friendly action deserving another.

She showered quickly and dressed, then went out into the living area, pausing only to pick up the sounds of Daniel moving about in his room before going to the kitchen.

By the time his door opened, and she heard his quick stride approaching, her preparations were complete.

She was aware of him halting in the doorway, clearly thrown by her presence in the kitchen at this hour, and turned, offering him a bright, friendly smile. 'Hi, I've made you some breakfast. Toast and coffee.'

He didn't smile back. 'I thought we had a ruling in place on that.'

'Well, yes, I suppose so. But I thought it would be a way of saying—thank you.' She paused. 'You were—very kind last night.'

'Really?' His mouth twisted sardonically. 'Now, I thought I was a bloody saint.'

'And I'm very grateful,' she added.

'I see,' he said. 'And am I supposed to pat you on the head and say, Anytime, darling? Because you can forget it.'

She bit her lip. 'You don't make it easy to be grateful.'

'I don't want it to be easy,' Dan said shortly. 'I'd prefer it to be unnecessary.'

She stared at him. 'I don't understand.'

'No? Then I'll explain. You really pushed your luck last night, sweetheart. To the limit. But try a trick like that again, and you won't get off so lightly.'

She said in a low voice, 'It wasn't intended as a trick. Truly it wasn't.'

'You mean that's your normal routine for nightmares—to invite the nearest available man to sleep with you but offer nothing in return?' he asked scornfully.

'It's never happened before…'

'And I suggest it never happens again.' He walked over to her, putting a hand under her chin, making her look up at him. 'Understand this, Laine. I'm not your brother, your guardian, your parent, or your maiden aunt. And when a woman asks me to bed I expect to have sex with her, not to be treated as if I was the resident bloody eunuch.'

The atmosphere between them seemed suddenly charged—resonant. The pressure of his fingers too intimate.

She jerked her chin away, forcing herself to return his hard gaze.

She said huskily, 'I apologise if I've insulted your manhood in some way. It was unintentional.' She paused. 'But you once said, if you remember, that you'd be content—to hold me, and ask for nothing else.'

'I remember only too well,' he said. 'It was my wedding night, and I thought I'd married a very young, very nervous, very innocent bride. But those criteria, of course, no longer apply— if they ever did. However, at the time I believed that some initial forbearance on my part would bring its own rewards. That before the honeymoon ended you'd be my wife—belong to me in absolute reality.'

And that's how it might have been if I hadn't read that letter, she thought. Laine, the blissful, besotted dupe, believing she was more than just a convenient body. I wonder when light would have dawned?

'Oh, dear.' She attempted a flippant note. 'How wrong is it possible to be?'

'With you, Laine,' he drawled, 'I'd say the margin for error stretches into infinity. And it's also occurred to me that, given your casual attitude to bedtime, your boyfriend might have felt justified in passing you on to this Clemmens guy.'

She went white. 'How dare you say that? You know nothing— *nothing*.' She drew a quivering breath. 'For God's sake, he was going to rape me.'

He shrugged cynically. 'Why didn't you try telling him you'd rather die than let him touch you? It worked for you the last time you were faced with a similar dilemma.'

She cried out and swung back her hand to slap his face—to hurt him in return. But only in a physical sense, because there'd be no breaking the emotional firewall he'd built around himself.

But Dan seized her wrist before she could make contact, holding it ruthlessly. 'No,' he told her grimly. 'You don't do that. Not now or ever.' He paused, adding reluctantly, 'But I shouldn't have said what I did. For what it's worth, I'm sorry.'

He let her go, and she leaned back against the work surface, looking at her wrist, at the marks his fingers had left, as she tried to control her breathing.

At last she said, 'Dan—about last night. There's probably no excuse except that you—used to be very kind to me, and I— suddenly needed kindness.'

'It's not hard to be kind to a lonely child,' he said quietly. 'Particularly when you've experienced the same situation.'

He paused, then added flatly, 'But you're not a child any more, Laine. You became a woman quite some time ago—on the night of your seventeenth birthday, as a matter of fact. I know, because I was there when it happened.'

And he turned and walked away, out of the kitchen and out of the flat, leaving her staring after him, her lips parted in shock.

CHAPTER NINE

IT MIGHT not have been the job she'd have chosen, but Laine was thankful to start work the following Monday morning.

Denise, her 'pair', was a considerably older woman, who whiled away the bus ride to the block of flats which would be the centre of their operations with a recital of her many and various ailments. She seemed remarkably robust for someone whose life had been despaired of so many times, Laine thought, her expression of polite interest pinned in place.

'I expect you go out clubbing at weekends, like all the youngsters,' Denise remarked, as she showed Laine round the basement where their cleaning materials and appliances were kept. 'But if you take my advice you'll start staying home and resting like me—if you want to be fit for Mondays.' She groaned. 'The times I've barely raised myself up.'

Far from socialising, Laine thought dryly, she'd spent the weekend alone, Daniel having left a curt message on the answering machine to say he would be away until late Sunday evening.

She found herself wondering wryly if he'd planned to be absent prior to her making an utter fool of herself the other night, and thought he probably hadn't.

All she knew for certain was that the flat seemed completely dead without him, and that she felt restless enough to scream.

The only interruption to her solitude had come from Jamie,

who'd called on Saturday evening but wanted to speak to Daniel, his exchanges with her being faintly perfunctory as a result.

She'd taken care to be in bed and asleep long before Daniel's return, whenever that had been, and out of the flat before he was awake this morning. Work, she hoped passionately, would give her something else to think about.

'Monday's always the hardest day, dear,' Denise was continuing, 'because they've all been at home for two days, making a mess.'

It seemed to Laine that most of the occupants of the flats led perfectly orderly lives. Denise, she thought, should have cleared up after her mother—or some of the clients on the boat.

And the flats themselves presented no particular problems. They'd been recently renovated to a very high standard, all wooden floors and clean lines—the minimalist look which would appeal to young professionals, as most of the tenants seemed to be.

'I thought you'd be too hoity-toity to get stuck in, but you're a good little worker, I'll say that for you,' Denise remarked as they ate their sandwiches at midday. 'Good and thorough. Where did you learn that?'

'I went on a crash course,' Laine said, blowing an inward kiss to Mrs Evershott. 'And the flats are easy to clean.'

Denise sniffed. 'I prefer a bit of comfort myself. A nice carpet, and proper curtains instead of those fiddly blinds.' She brightened. 'When I started I used to work about a mile away, in Greenlaw Mansions. Now, they were *really* luxurious—like palaces, most of them, and big with it. Took some keeping up, I can tell you.'

Yes, Laine thought. I know. I thought I was going to live in one of them once with the man I loved. Before we found a house. Made a real home together.

And swiftly changed the subject.

She was bone-weary at the end of the day, but at least she knew now what was expected, and was confident she could stay on top of the work.

She'd cooked a small beef joint the previous night, and had the remainder cold with salad for supper.

The evening wore on, with no sign of Dan, and if this was going to be the shape of her days then she had no choice but to live with it.

After all, she supposed wearily as she trailed into her room, she only had herself to blame.

Yet she couldn't put his parting words from her mind.

How much, she thought, had she betrayed of her feelings in those few delirious seconds when she was seventeen? Enough, probably, to suggest that she was his for the taking—if he wanted her. And that, shamefully, he wouldn't even have to try too hard.

Which must have made her total rejection of him a double shock. And, anyway, being turned down at all would have been a new and unwelcome experience for him, she thought, her lips twisting painfully.

She found herself wondering suddenly why Candida had delayed so long in showing her the letter. Why hadn't she produced it as soon as Daniel proposed, or at least in the run-up to the wedding, when not so much harm would have been done?

Apart, she thought, sighing, from my heart, which would still have broken.

But Daniel would have survived with his pride only slightly dented if

I'd backed out before the ceremony. Far better to find out now, friends would have told him, before it's too late. That's what engagements are for.

As it was, there was small wonder that his anger and bitterness had not perceptibly faded.

But I, she thought, have reason to be bitter too. So why do I seem to feel nothing but a regret that goes beyond tears?

Days passed, and work became a not-too-testing routine. Home life, however, was another matter altogether, with Daniel seeming to spend less time than ever at the flat.

I come in, he goes out, and vice versa, Laine thought. We're like the men and women in those little weather houses—only one of us visible at a time.

And when they did encounter one another he was coolly civil, with no sign that he'd ever experienced any stronger emotions towards her.

I'd almost rather he was angry again, she thought with a pang. At least then I'd feel he was actually *seeing* me.

Soon, she supposed, his house—wherever it was—would be ready for him, and he'd be moving out altogether. And she would never see him again. Perhaps, in time, she'd even stop thinking about him—stop wanting him.

But, looking on what passed for the bright side, at least she didn't have housework to face all over again when she returned in the evening, Daniel having arbitrarily changed Mrs Archer's hours so that she was now coming to the flat on a daily basis.

'Fastidious gentleman, that,' the good woman had commented to a startled Laine, at the start of the new regime. 'Clean sheets and towels every day, and his shirts having to be ironed just so. Funny to think of him being Mr James's friend.' She added hastily, 'Of course, miss, I don't mean to imply...'

But Laine had laughed. 'It's all right, Mrs Archer. You don't have to spare my feelings. I know my brother would make a troll seem fussy.'

However, she had challenged Daniel on his return that night. 'You might have consulted me over Mrs Archer. She is supposed to be a shared expense, and I can't afford to pay any more for her services.'

'You don't have to. She's here for my convenience, not yours.'

'So I gather.' She turned away. 'Providing an endless supply of clean sheets, no less. How hedonistic.'

He shrugged. 'One of life's last great luxuries,' he retorted. 'Why shouldn't I indulge myself?'

'No reason at all,' she said colourlessly. 'You're very fortunate that you've always been able to buy everything you want.'

'No,' he said. 'Not everything, darling, if you remember.' He paused. 'Perhaps you weren't the only one to make a mistake two years ago, Laine. Maybe I made one too.' His voice was hard-edged with derision. 'Was that it? Did I fail to offer a high enough price for your favours? You should have said so at the time, and we could have—reopened negotiations.'

She bit back the instinctive cry of pain—of negation. Lifted her chin and met his gaze without outward flinching.

'You seem to forget,' she said, keeping her voice even, 'that I turned down all offers of a settlement from you. So it was never—ever—about money.'

'What, then? What brought about the change? Because there was one.'

Daniel spoke harshly, urgently, his eyes never leaving hers. 'Or did you think I'd also forgotten the way you once came into my arms—how your body trembled against mine—the taste of your lips? You wanted me, damn you.'

She was trembling again—quaking inside—realising she'd been only too right about that brief but telling moment of self-betrayal.

'Yes,' she said defiantly. 'I admit it—I was tempted. Once. How could I not be? You were the most glamorous, sexy guy I'd ever met. A young girl's dream. But dreams don't last, and fortunately I woke up just in time, with no harm done.'

He said with cold grimness, 'How interesting you should think so.' And walked away into his room, slamming the door behind him.

Well, Laine thought, sinking her teeth into a lower lip, at least that's one conversation we'll never need to have again.

And wished, quietly and desperately, that she could find it more of a consolation.

'What's going on?' Laine demanded. 'Why can't we pass?'

It was the middle of her third week with Citi-Clean, and she'd arrived for work with Denise to find the entire street cordoned off, choked by police cars and other emergency vehicles.

'They won't say.' Denise had gone to enquire and come puffing back in high excitement. 'Just that there's been an incident, and no one's being allowed in or out. But they did say that the road probably won't be cleared until at least this afternoon, and that we shouldn't hang around waiting.'

She paused. 'I suppose I'd better phone Old Mother Moss—give her the bad news. But we've got a morning off, gal. So enjoy it, because as soon as the police give the word Mrs M will have us back in those flats, working until all hours.'

I'm glad to hear it, because I could do with less leisure, not more, Laine thought as she went home. I'd rather work all day, go home dog-tired, and fall asleep without thinking. Find a place where this slow, grinding ache of need inside me can finally sink into oblivion and give me a few hours' peace.

She hadn't slept well the previous night. Something had disturbed her—voices, somewhere—probably in the street below. And afterwards, she'd been restless, with the result that she hadn't responded immediately to her alarm clock when it sounded, and had been forced to rush.

As usual, Dan had already left. Unusually, however, he'd left the living room untidy—a used glass on the table and sofa cushions tossed to the floor. Well, Mrs Archer could deal with that, she'd thought as she fled. She didn't have time.

Yet here she was now, with unexpected time on her hands and no idea what to do with it.

As she unlocked the front door and went into the flat she became instantly aware of sounds coming from the kitchen. The chink of crockery, she realised. The opening and closing of cupboard doors.

She halted, surprised and a little startled, because it was too early for Mrs Archer, who usually arrived around midday. Unless, of course, Dan had changed her hours again.

But it wasn't a middle-aged cleaning lady who emerged from the kitchen, but someone she'd never seen before. A girl with a mane of silvery fair hair spilling over her shoulders, who was wearing one of Dan's shirts and nothing else, judging by the amount of expensive golden tan she was revealing. A girl with enormous blue eyes, full lips, and legs that went on for ever.

She checked too, when she saw Laine, her blue eyes widening as they absorbed the navy uniform dress, with the prominent Citi-Clean logo just above the right breast.

'Oh,' she said. 'Are you the maid? Dan didn't mention you'd be turning up.'

He didn't mention you either, thought Laine, feeling almost sick with shock, her eyes flicking involuntarily to the still displaced sofa cushions. And last night's voices hadn't been in the street, but right here. And thank God I didn't get up to investigate, because who knows what I might have walked in on?

She found a voice from somewhere. Not one that she particularly recognised, but it would do. 'Actually, I live here. But I work for a maid service somewhere else.'

'I see,' the girl said doubtfully, then smiled, her face lighting up with swift charm. 'No, frankly, I *don't* see. I can't get my head round any of this. Daniel Flynn—flat-sharing? Unbelievable. And a place like this too.' She paused, flushing a little. 'I'm sorry. That sounds horribly rude, and I'm sure it's really nice in its way, but it's just—not Dan's kind of territory.'

'I agree,' Laine said evenly. 'It seems like he's slumming to me, too. But I wasn't around when he did the deal with my brother.' She paused. 'Perhaps he didn't explain that he—he's an old friend of the family. And this is strictly a temporary arrangement while the renovations on his house are being completed.' She added stiltedly, 'Of course you know he's bought a house?'

'Oh, please let's not go there.' The girl groaned comically. 'Morning, noon and night I hear nothing but complaints about builders, delays, supplies, penalty clauses. The whole bit. You must be sick of it too.'

'Daniel and I just share a roof,' Laine said quietly. 'I'm not in his confidence.'

And I know nothing about you either, she thought, except that you're the current update on the usual model—like his cars. But, then, why should I know? The only real surprise here is that it's never happened before. Why I should have assumed he'd continue to play away instead of bringing his girls back here. After all, he has no reason to spare my feelings—even if he knew they existed.

'Oh,' the girl said slowly. 'Well—I'm Belinda. And I'm also in real trouble. Because Dan made me swear I'd be out of here by now—only, like an idiot, I went back to sleep.' She shrugged, her expression rueful—conspiratorial. 'You know how it is.'

No, Laine returned silently, the ache inside her twisting into quiet agony. I don't know, and I never have.

'I thought I'd make myself a drink before I went in the shower,' Belinda continued. 'I was hoping there'd be some herb tea around, but I can't find any.'

'There should be some camomile,' Laine said steadily. 'Try the last cupboard to the right of the stove.'

'Terrific.' Belinda lingered, her glance questioning. 'Would you like some, too—er…?'

Laine forced her mouth into the approximation of a smile. 'It's Laine,' she said. 'Laine Sinclair, and I'll pass on the tea, thanks.'

'Fine.' The other shrugged again. 'Then, I'll—see you later.' And she disappeared back into the kitchen, allowing Laine to escape into her bedroom.

Moving like an automaton, she removed her uniform and put it on a hanger, then wrapped herself in her old robe and lay down on the bed, aware that she was shivering.

I can't go on like this, she thought. I can't bear it

Knowing that something must be so is one thing, but being confronted head-on by the evidence is quite another. And his Belinda seems really nice. In other circumstances I might have liked her, wanted to get to know her better.

As it is…

She turned over, burying her face in her pillow. And when,

some time later, she heard a soft tap on the door and Belinda saying, 'Laine, I just wanted to let you know I'm leaving now,' she made no reply.

Denise, she found, had been correct in her prediction. By mid-afternoon they were both back in uniform and back at the flats, making up the lost hours.

'It'll mean overtime,' Denise said. 'But that won't stop my old man playing hell. He expects me there when he gets home.' She paused. 'Got anyone waiting for you, gal?'

'No,' Laine said. 'No one at all.'

But in this instance she was wrong, because when she got back to the flat, just after nine-thirty in the evening, Daniel was there, pacing up and down, his face like thunder.

'Where the hell have you been?' he demanded, swinging round as she entered. He was barefoot, his casual black shirt hanging open over a pair of close-fitting jeans. He looked bad-tempered and incredibly sexy—as if he'd just fallen out of bed, she thought, wondering whether he'd spent the evening alone, or Belinda had come back. If so, she was not there now, and Laine despised herself for the relief that flooded her.

Daniel thrust the evening paper at her. 'Have you seen this?' He read the headline aloud. '"Drug dealer shot in Kensington slaying." And right where you work, Laine. You could have been in the middle of it. I've been worried sick.'

'Then don't be.' She glared back at him. 'It was over when I got there, and all it meant was a later start and an even later finish.' She paused. 'And, in any case, it's no damned business of yours.'

'Don't be so bloody silly.' His voice was rough. 'I'm bound to be concerned.'

'No,' she said with equal fierceness. 'You're not. You have no obligations towards me in any way at all—as I decided a long time ago.'

'What are you talking about?'

'Nothing.' She cursed herself silently for the tiredness that had caused that slip of the tongue. 'You said it yourself—you're not my brother or any other relation. Please remember that, and get off my case.'

She bit her lip. 'Also, I've had a swine of a day,' she added chokingly.

'So I really don't need to be shouted at—especially by you. I just want to have a bath and go to bed—if that's quite all right?'

There was a taut silence, then he said, 'Have you eaten?'

She could hardly remember. 'No,' she admitted reluctantly. 'Not lately.'

'Then go and have your bath, and I'll make supper for you.'

She looked down at the carpet. 'Be careful,' she said in a low voice. 'That sounds dangerously like kindness again.'

His mouth twisted. 'I'll risk it if you will. Now, be off with you before I start shouting again.'

She got to her bedroom door, then turned as a thought struck her. 'Anyway, how did you know the area I worked?'

'I wrote you a reference.' He shrugged. 'It made sense to find out what kind of outfit it was and what was involved.'

She stared at him. '*You* wrote it—yourself?'

'Isn't that what you asked me to do?'

'Why—yes.' But she'd assumed that he'd hand the task on to his secretary, as he'd told her.

'Well, then.' His voice slowed to a drawl. 'And I suggest you go—unless you want me to run your bath for you, and put you in it?'

She caught her breath on a startled gasp, then shot into her room, closing the door behind her with emphasis. From temper to teasing, she thought in bewilderment. So what mood would he be in next? And how safe would it be to find out?

She stood for a moment, staring into space, then shook her head, telling herself she was overreacting, and went into the bathroom, shedding her clothes on the way.

She half filled the tub, sinking down into the water with a

small sigh of pleasure as she closed her eyes, yet aware at the same time that complete relaxation was beyond her.

Knowing that he'd been on her mind all day, her strenuous mopping, vacuuming and polishing punctuated by images of him and Belinda together, making love, leaving her struggling between shame and misery.

And where Daniel was concerned she didn't have to imagine a thing. Not since that day she'd walked back into the flat and met him, strolling naked out of her bedroom. One more memory among the many she was unable to blot from her consciousness.

But then everything that had occurred between them was in the past, she thought. No present, and certainly no future— unless, somehow, she made it happen.

She slid further down into the water, thinking unwillingly of Belinda, the golden—the beautiful—and curved in all the right places, as revealed by that inadequately fastened shirt. And then looked down at herself.

Not just slim—she could almost count her ribs. Her breasts were reasonably shaped, but small, and her hipbones were altogether too prominent.

No wonder Daniel had seen her as a child, to be treated with kindness and forbearance.

But that wasn't enough. Not then. Not now.

Living with him, she thought, but not living together. Loving him, but always being forced to hide it. To accept loneliness and isolation, and at the same time to conceal the longing that crucified her—and now the jealousy.

Ever since their wedding night she'd walked a tightrope between misery on one hand and pride on the other. But now her balance was slipping, and she couldn't guarantee how much longer she could remain in control of her emotions. Of the physical needs she'd tried to ignore over the requirements of sheer survival.

Only that wasn't working any more—creating a problem she knew she wasn't experienced enough to solve.

And to begin with she had to go back into the living room,

and sit with him, eating whatever food he'd prepared, and appearing grateful but not overwhelmed. When all the time…

She dried herself slowly and dressed in another of her collection of anonymous white blouses and an ankle-length green skirt that she'd bought originally for her honeymoon and worn rarely since.

Certainly Dan had never seen it, or much of her trousseau at all—apart from the yellow dress he'd claimed he wanted to unbutton, creating at least an illusion of desire for his girl-bride.

And, of course, her nightgown.

But she doubted whether he'd noticed that, because by then he'd only been looking at her face, searching her eyes, focussing on the movement of her lips as they spoke the words that would drive him away from her.

Words that still rankled with him. Words that he would never forgive, but which might prove her salvation. Might prevent her from throwing away her hard-won pride in some ludicrous attempt to make him see her as a woman—even for only a few hours. One night out of his life and hers, she thought with sudden yearning. Was that really so much to ask?

And knew that it was. That it had to be. That anything else was unthinkable.

Therefore she left her small store of cosmetics in their bag, so that it wouldn't look as if she was making any special effort, and instead simply brushed her hair until it curved to her shoulders before she went to join him.

Daniel was stretched out on one of the sofas, watching some news programme on television and drinking wine when she came in, and she felt his eyes flicker over her in swift appraisal as he rose and handed her the glass he'd filled for her too.

He said laconically, 'Supper's on its way,' and disappeared into the kitchen.

She sat down on the other sofa, curling bare toes into the rug as she sipped her wine, feeling its coolness refresh her dry mouth. At the same time she noticed the small dining table had only been set with a place for one.

'You're not eating?' she queried when he returned a few minutes later, carrying a plate.

'I had an early business dinner,' he said. 'Come and eat this while it's hot.'

'This,' she discovered, was a mound of perfectly scrambled eggs, sprinkled with tiny slivers of smoked salmon and accompanied by fingers of golden toast.

'It's amazing,' she said after the first forkful. 'I had no idea you could cook.'

He brought his glass and the bottle to the table and sat down. His voice was dry. 'I suspect the things that we don't know about each other could fill a medium-sized book.'

When she'd finished, she sat back with a sigh of contentment. 'If you'd asked me, I'd have said I was too tired to eat.'

'How about talking?' he said. 'Are you too tired for that?'

Laine fiddled with the stem of her glass. 'That—rather depends on the topic of conversation.'

'Not an easy one, I fear.' His tone was blunt. 'I want to know how much money your former boyfriend took from you down in Florida. Jamie reckons he cleaned you out.'

She flushed. 'Jamie should not have discussed it, and you had no right to ask him.'

'I was here when you woke up screaming.' He spoke calmly. 'So let's not talk about rights.'

'But I wasn't screaming over the damage to my bank balance.' She drank some more wine. 'Over being a fool, perhaps. But that's all over and done with, and I have to forget it and move on.'

'Except you seem to be moving backwards.' He took her hand, inspecting the small square palm and the slim fingers with their blunt unvarnished nails, running the ball of his thumb over their faint roughness.

Making her recall his teasing comment about having soft hands for their honeymoon and pull away, her blush deepening.

'Just don't tell me you've opted for Spain after all,' he went on, his glance faintly sardonic. 'Although I gather the golfing life didn't work out, and your mother's now in Portugal.'

'It was Mr Tanfield who didn't work out,' she said. 'But Mother's fallen on her feet, apparently—found a rich widower who adores her.'

'You don't have much contact with her?'

She shook her head. 'Jamie suspects she's knocked a few years off her age, and grown-up children wouldn't fit the legend.'

Daniel's brows lifted. 'She's all heart,' he said dryly. He paused. 'So what are your long-term plans, Laine?'

'How odd,' she said. 'I was going to ask you exactly the same. You—your house must be nearly ready by now?'

'Getting there.' Dan refilled his glass. His smile was hard. 'You really can't wait to be rid of me, can you, darling?'

'I'd have thought you'd be equally keen to go,' she returned. 'To have your own space—your privacy again.' She looked down at the polished surface of the table. 'Be honest, Dan. You'd never have taken on this flat if you'd thought for one minute that I'd suddenly turn up here.'

'No,' he agreed reflectively. 'Probably not.'

'So,' she said. 'Have you a moving date yet?'

'Nothing settled.' He paused. 'In fact, I'm no longer sure I'm going to live in the house even when it is finally finished. I may simply sell it on.'

She remembered Belinda's discontented words. Wondered if she was the reason for this change of heart. She said steadily, 'Builders, delays, supplies, penalty clauses. I suppose all that can be a turn-off—in certain circumstances.'

'But you don't have to worry,' he said. 'Whatever happens, I've decided not to stay on here any longer. As soon as I find somewhere else I'll be gone.'

Gone, Laine thought. A small word, short and sharp, like a bullet through the head. And as final.

'Well,' she heard herself say, as she picked up her plate and set off with it to the kitchen, 'that's—good.'

She hadn't expected him to follow, or to lounge in the doorway as she washed up and scrubbed out the pan.

'A muted reception of such momentous news,' he commented. 'I thought you'd be jumping for joy.' He paused. 'And you don't ask why I'm going.'

Because I already know. I've seen her—talked to her. Can see why you'd want to find somewhere new and perfect to share with her.

She shrugged. 'It's not my business.'

There was a silence, then Dan said quietly, 'Has it really been so bad?'

Worse than you could ever imagine, she cried out in her heart. *And worst of all will be watching you leave and knowing that this time it's for ever. That you'll never hold me again, even in kindness.*

That I'll never know what it's like to be kissed in passion by you—touched...

And that there isn't enough pride in the whole world to compensate for that. For the aching void my life will become without you—without ever having known you. Belonged to you—for just one night.

'No,' she said. 'Really, you've been—very considerate.'

He said bleakly, 'I seem to specialise in that,' and turned back into the living room.

So what do I do? Laine asked herself when she was alone. How do I choose between one lifetime of regret and another?

All I know is that I want him more than life itself, and I'll never forgive myself if I don't take this last chance—and try, just once, to make him want me in return. To prove that I'm not a child.

Even if I don't know where—or how—to begin to be a woman. But, whatever the cost, it has to be worth it. To be—just briefly—his wife at last.

And have it to remember—always.

CHAPTER TEN

How on earth, Laine asked herself, did you go about seducing a man? Especially one who was sitting staring into space, his face brooding and his mouth set, apparently not even aware that you'd deliberately sat down next to him instead of choosing a seat on the other side of the room, as he might have expected.

She reached for her refilled glass and took a substantial gulp. Dutch courage—of which she might need every scrap.

She drew a deep breath. 'It's strange, isn't it? That we should start talking to each other now—just when you're about to leave.'

'Did we talk?' Daniel asked abruptly. 'It seemed to me we only skirted round the edges of a few no-go areas.'

'We could always—try again.' She paused. 'For instance, you asked if Andy cleaned me out. Yes, he did. But perhaps that wasn't the worst of it.'

'No,' he said. 'He left you to the mercies of some other bastard.' He added harshly. 'Unforgivable.'

'That's a terrible word,' she said with swift vehemence. 'Everyone deserves a little forgiveness. Because sometimes you can't help what you do,' she went on, remembering in spite of herself the look on his face when he'd left her that terrible night two years before. 'When you're in trouble, and your life is falling to pieces around you, then you have to try and save yourself— whatever the means.'

She added in a low voice, 'And if you hurt someone you can only hope with all your heart that they'll understand one day why you were forced to do it.'

And waited—wondering if he would indeed understand what she was trying to say.

But Daniel only smiled cynically. 'I think most of us are rather too human for that, Lily Maid.'

'Don't call me that,' she said passionately. 'It—it's a childish name.'

'And probably inappropriate for other reasons too,' Daniel drawled. 'My apologies, Miss Sinclair.'

She bit her lip. Of course he thought she'd slept with Andy. That she'd only rejected him, not other men. And she'd have to let him think so. Because if she told him she was still a virgin it could prompt some awkward questions.

She said, 'Can I ask you a question?'

'What do you want to know?'

When you leave here, are you moving in with Belinda? Are you going to marry her?

No, she thought. Not that. Because you might not like the answer.

A different query pushed itself forward from some deep corner of her mind, where it had lain almost forgotten. Almost but not quite.

She heard herself say, 'Did my mother want you to sleep with her?'

His appalled expression as he turned to her was genuine. His hasty, 'No, of course not,' was less convincing.

She said, 'You can tell me the truth, Dan. I'm a big girl now.'

His hands descended on her shoulders, gripping them without gentleness. 'What the hell has she been saying?' His voice was hoarse with urgency. 'My God—did that lying bitch actually dare tell you I took her to bed? Is that why—?'

'No,' she said. 'No, I promise you she didn't. In fact, I had the opposite impression. It was just a passing remark, but it left me wondering, that's all.'

His hands fell away from her. She saw a muscle move in his throat as he swallowed. He said stiltedly, 'I'm sorry. I shouldn't have spoken about her like that. Let's just say it was one of life's more embarrassing moments for both of us, and leave it there.'

He paused. 'Now can I ask *you* something?'

'I—suppose.'

'Why did you marry me, Laine, and then refuse to be my wife?'

She'd known it must come. Had prepared for it. She said quietly, 'Because I realised that, however good one's intentions may be, you can't simply command love to exist. Not the real kind—the way two people should feel about each other if they're going to spend their life together.' She took a deep breath. 'And when I understood that I knew I couldn't bear a marriage that was just a cheat. And that I had to stop it.'

'Just like that?' he asked harshly. 'Without giving me a chance to try and make you happy?'

'But you couldn't have done that.' She didn't look at him. 'I'd have had to pretend. And how long could that possibly have lasted?'

He was silent for a moment, then he said bleakly, 'I asked for honesty, so I can hardly complain when I get it.' He glanced at his watch and rose. 'I have an early start tomorrow, so I'll say goodnight.'

It was now or never. As he turned away, she reached up and took his hand, halting him. 'Daniel, before you go, will you kiss me?'

He looked down at her. 'Laine—I don't need a bloody consolation prize.'

'And that's not what I'm offering.' She rose too, and moved to him, sliding her arms round him under the open shirt, flattening the palms of her hands against the hard muscles of his back. 'Please, Dan,' she whispered, and all the months and years of longing sounded in her voice. 'Please kiss me.'

For a moment he hesitated, then slowly bent his head and took her mouth with his. It was the lightest of pressures, but she felt the kiss quiver through every nerve-ending in her body.

Involuntarily, she pressed closer to him, letting the taut peaks of her breasts, proud under their thin cotton covering, brush the warmth of his bare chest as her lips parted beneath his, inviting a deeper and more intimate possession.

For a moment he responded, the silken glide of his tongue meeting hers, then with startling abruptness it was over, and Dan was lifting his head, putting her away from him, his hands gripping her shoulders as he held her at arm's length. He looked at her unsmilingly.

'What's going on, Laine?' he asked. 'What game are we playing here?'

'I don't know what you mean.'

'I mean I'm the same man that you couldn't bear to have near you—whose touch disgusted you. What's suddenly changed?'

'Perhaps I have.' She hesitated. 'Dan—it was a long time ago.'

'Strange,' he said. 'I remember it as if it was yesterday.'

She swallowed. 'And—because of that—you don't want me now?'

Oh, God, she thought, the ultimate humiliation. And she'd asked for it.

'On the contrary,' Daniel drawled. 'The idea of you, naked and willing in my bed at last, has an appeal all its own. But the scale of your previous rejection makes me—wary. I'm sure you can understand that. So, what do you want from me, Laine?'

'I—I don't know.' It was pathetic, but it was also the truth. That door in her life was still waiting to open.

'Then maybe you should think it over carefully and decide,' he said. 'Before you risk making another terrible mistake.' He paused then added grimly, 'Because if I get to the point of no return with you, and find you've changed your mind again, I shall not take it well. Don't say you weren't warned.'

He released her and turned, walking towards his room.

'Daniel.' It was almost a whisper. 'Stay with me, please. Don't go.' *Hold me again. Kiss me until I stop thinking…*

At his door, he paused and looked back at her. 'I'm not going far, Laine. And if you decide you want me, you know where to find me.' He added evenly, 'But if you come to me, by God you'd better mean it.' His mouth twisted. 'However, I shan't hold my breath.'

His door closed and he left her standing alone in the middle of the room, fingers pressed to her tingling lips.

She thought, almost wildly, I can't do this. I can't just— present myself to him, as if I was some slave girl going to the Sultan. He can't expect that...

And stopped. Because that was it, she realised. He didn't expect it—or anything else from her. He thought she'd forget whatever passing madness had taken her into his arms just now, and opt for her own bed and safety.

Probably I am mad, she thought, as she went into her room. But I have a long, lonely time ahead of me to be sane.

The nightgown she'd bought for her wedding night was still there, wrapped in tissue and pushed to the back of a drawer. She'd always meant to throw it away, but never quite managed it. Now she knew why.

It floated round her like a delicate cloud as she crossed to his room and opened the door.

One of the bedside lamps was switched on, but Daniel was lying motionless with his back to the door. For a moment she thought he was asleep.

Not waiting for her. Expecting nothing.

Then he turned slowly, almost reluctantly, and looked at her, propping himself on an elbow.

He said softly, 'Are you quite sure?'

For answer, she slid her hands under the straps of her nightgown, pushing them off her shoulders so that the mist of fabric slipped silently to the floor.

Naked, she thought, *as he wanted. But her willingness might depend on him—and whether past anger outweighed present desire. Something which only he could decide.*

He was very still, staring at her as if he could not believe what his eyes were telling him. Then suddenly he moved, throwing back the covers and striding round the bed to her, lithe as a panther.

He took her in his arms, his hard nakedness against hers, his hand tangling in her hair, tipping her head back as he kissed her for the first time in heated sensual demand, bruising her lips, his tongue a flame in her mouth. His hands moved slowly, commandingly, down her body, from throat to thigh, in a gesture of total possession.

Then, still kissing her, he picked her up and carried her to the bed.

'Aren't you going to switch off the lamp?' When she could finally speak, her voice was a husky thread.

'No, I want to see your eyes,' he whispered back as he bent over her, his hands moving in languorous enjoyment over her throat, her shoulders and down, brushing her breasts with such tantalising grace that a small, helpless sound was forced from her. 'To know that you like what I'm doing.'

'I'd tell you…'

'You could fib.' His fingers were cupping her breasts, his thumbs moving lazily, circling the rosy peaks, making them swell and harden under the enticement of his touch.

'I wouldn't…' She choked the denial.

'You mean you've never faked an orgasm?' His lips smiled against the pulse in her throat. 'You must be unique.'

And if ever there was a time to confess that she'd never experienced orgasm, or any of the other bewildering delights being revealed to her starved and restless body, it was right then and there.

Except that it was already too late. Because his mouth had moved downwards now, and he was kissing her breasts, his tongue curling round her erect nipples, creating such helpless, excruciating pleasure that this time she could only manage an incoherent whimper as she arched towards him.

'Yes, sweetheart,' he whispered, as if she'd asked a rational question. 'But let's take it easy, shall we? Because there's no hurry—no hurry at all.'

And she believed him, as she sank, yielding, into his embrace.

He was exploring her entire body with his fingertips, learning her inch by inch, every line and each curve, as if he was blind and she was the landscape he must discover in order to survive. Turning her in his arms so he could trace the long, shivering curve of her spine, the soft swell of her buttocks. And where his hands touched, his lips followed.

And sometimes he spoke to her, his voice sinking to a husky murmur as he told her how lovely she was, describing the texture of her skin, its scent, its taste, with a mesmerising candour that should have embarrassed her but instead made her burn and shiver with excitement.

She was shy of him only once, when his mouth began to caress the little silky triangle at the joining of her thighs, his purpose intimately apparent, and she told him 'No', in a small cracked voice she did not even recognise.

'Let's say—not yet,' he whispered, and began to kiss her mouth again, moving a little, so that she felt the length, the hardness of him pressing against her as his hand slid between her legs, stroking her slick, hot wetness, his long fingers moving on her, inside her, with exquisite thoroughness, until she was writhing under his caresses, pleading without words as she gasped against his lips.

Until the moment he lifted himself over her, guided himself into her, and her gasp suddenly became one of pain as she flinched away from him in shock and disbelief. Because she'd never expected it to hurt—how could it when she wanted him so much? And yet it did.

He stopped instantly. Waited. 'Laine?' Her name was a question, demanding an answer. Then, in the same moment, the pain was gone—but so was he, pulling out of her to lie beside her, not touching her, his face buried in the pillow as he struggled to control his ragged breathing.

Laine turned away, curling herself into a ball, closing her eyes as she whispered, 'I'm sorry—I'm so sorry,' because she could think of nothing else to say. Because she'd wanted so desperately to please him, to be everything he wanted. Instead she'd turned—once again—into this hideous disappointment at the mercy of her own inadequacies.

'Sorry?' His voice was husky, incredulous. 'What are you talking about?'

'I thought it was just an old wives' tale.' Her voice was a small wretched mumble. 'I didn't think it could happen—not to me. That I could be so unlucky.'

She felt his hand on her shoulder, soothing her damp skin, quietening her sudden uncontrollable trembling. 'Laine, look at me.'

She turned slowly to face him, lifting reluctant eyelids.

He said gently, 'There are old husbands' tales too, about the astonishing thrill of knowing that the girl in your arms has never belonged to anyone else. I didn't believe them either. Until now. And I don't feel even slightly unlucky.'

She said, faltering a little. 'But you haven't—'

He laid a silencing finger on her lips. 'And nor have you,' he told her softly. 'But you will, and so shall I. That's a promise.'

He wrapped his arms round her and they lay quietly together, Daniel dropping gentle kisses on her hair, her forehead and her eyes, tiny contacts that made her skin tingle with the beginning of renewed arousal, until she reached up, drawing him down to the soft eagerness of her parted lips.

As his hands resumed their seductive journey over her skin, she sighed, stretching the entire length of her body against his, feeling once more, in the throb of her pulses, the glow of her quickening blood.

He fondled her breasts softly and voluptuously, turning them to aching delight under his touch. And she lifted herself towards him, glorying in the balm of his lips and tongue as he caressed the swollen mounds, then tasted the fragrance of her own skin as his mouth returned to hers, kissing her deeply and lingeringly.

But when at last his questing hands reached her thighs Laine felt herself tense involuntarily.

'Relax, sweetheart,' he whispered, his mouth tender on hers. 'I'm not going to hurt you. Not again.'

And slowly she surrendered, allowing him the access he was seeking, hiding the warmth of her face in his shoulder as he caressed her.

His touch was different this time, delicate, but infinitely sure, like the subtle friction of silk on silk, as he sought and found her tiny female bud, brushing it gently with his fingertips, creating the merest whisper of sensation at first, then slowly increasing the pressure, persuading it into throbbing, startled tumescence, and beyond.

Taking her to a place where the sheer delight of this sensual teasing drew close to torment. Making the bewildered breath catch in her throat as she felt her control began to slip from her, became aware she was approaching a brink that she had not known existed until this moment. Until this driven, spiralling moment that possessed her utterly, transcending all else in its sheer intensity.

That lifted her to some peak, held her there endlessly—then released her in a sunburst of amazed pleasure, her entire body convulsing in one exquisite spasm after another.

And as she cried out against his skin, bemused by joy, his hands slid under her, lifting her to him, and this time her rapturous body's moist inner heat offered no resistance to the smooth, powerful thrust that made her his.

For a while Dan remained still, holding her, kissing her, murmuring reassurance as her quivering senses swam down from the heights he'd guided her to. Until, eventually, she was ready for the new and astonishing reality of his body sheathed inside her, and the gentle rocking of his loins against hers.

Until she realised too that this quiet, subtle motion was already having its own insidious effect, creating other extraordinary and quite enchanting sensations that were demanding her renewed concentration.

So that her own body was not merely adapting itself to these new circumstances but becoming dizzily, gladly accepting of every warm, vibrant inch of him. Even, she thought dazedly, wanting more.

That, as a result, her hands were sliding up to lock at the back of his neck as their mouths met and clung, lips and tongues meshing in unrestrained urgency and need. And that, at the same time, some instinct was urging her to raise her legs and clasp them round his hips.

Then, as if some switch had been thrown, Daniel moved, arching himself above her, his former languor forgotten as he began to thrust into her, slowly and rhythmically at first, each driving movement seeming to carry him ever more deeply inside her, then more swiftly and forcefully.

And she went with him, caught suddenly and helplessly in the irresistible tide that was sweeping her away. Aware that her body, incredibly, was responding once more. That from some unknown core, buried far down inside her, she could feel the first stirrings of a pleasure that she could now recognise and welcome. That she could consciously seek after. And that she could not allow to escape her.

And he was speaking, telling her, his voice hoarse and shaken, that it was now—it had to be now—and that she must—she must...

Gasping, sobbing in her throat, she reached for ecstasy with her whole being and felt its first harsh pulsations tear though her as he cried out in turn, the sound ripped from him, as his body shuddered into its own fierce, seething climax.

Afterwards there was silence. Daniel lay slumped and still against her, his head pillowed on her breasts, his body still joined to hers.

Eventually he stirred, peeling himself slowly and reluctantly away from her, and she realised he was getting out of bed, and crossing to the bathroom where, a moment later, she heard the shower running.

Laine stayed where she was, drained and boneless, but realising as the minutes passed that the euphoria which had brought her floating down from the heights was beginning to fade under the onset of reality.

Daniel might have shown her heaven, but there was no promise of lasting bliss. This was no bridal night—just a girl having sex with a man, and wholly at her own instigation, too.

She bit her lip, wondering what she should do now—whether there was some post-coital etiquette that should be observed.

Should Daniel's departure be regarded as a signal for her to return to her own room?

But as she turned to look for her discarded nightgown Daniel came back, unselfconsciously naked, and carrying a towel and a sponge.

He sat on the edge of the bed and drew back the covers, frowning faintly as he looked down at her, and Laine, following his glance, realised there was a tiny smear of blood on her thighs.

'Oh, no.' Her voice was a small wail of embarrassment, as swiftly and gently he sponged the mark away and handed her the towel. 'I—I'm so sorry.'

'I'm the one who should be feeling guilty,' Daniel said wryly, wrapping the damp sponge in the towel, and putting it on the floor. He smoothed a strand of hair back from her face. 'Sweetheart, did I hurt you very badly?'

She tried to smile. 'I don't think I remember.' Adding hurriedly, 'Now I'd better let you get some sleep.'

'Great idea.' He turned off the lamp and slid back under the covers, drawing her against him, settling her in his arms.

'You—want me to stay?' She was still unsure.

'Of course.' She could hear a smile in his voice. 'You're not supposed to kiss and run, you know. Besides, having had your evil way with me, the least you can do is spend the night.'

She whispered, 'Yes,' and turned her face into the warm, familiar scent of his shoulder. He fell asleep almost at once, and she lay listening to the quiet, regular sound of his breathing, wishing that she could do the same.

But if her body was weary her mind was wide-awake, filled

with fleeting thoughts and images, making her move restlessly, uncomfortably.

'Can't you sleep?' His voice reached her softly.

'It doesn't seem so. I—I didn't mean to disturb you.'

'Don't worry about it. Maybe there's something I can do to help.' He paused. 'A hot drink, perhaps? Or a lullaby? Or even—this.'

He shifted slightly, adjusting his position and hers, and she gave a little gasp of surprise and pleasure as he entered her— filled her once more.

It was almost like dreaming. A time of small delicious, unforgettable intensities. A tenderness of lips and fingertips. And an unhurried, lingering edging towards ultimate and mutual delight.

And a little astonished sob broke in her throat as her body shivered and fragmented into orgasm. And after rapture came peace, and Laine, sighing, drifted into slumber at last, in her lover's arms.

The next time she opened her eyes it was daylight, and she was alone. Not just in bed, either. The silence told her that Dan had left for the day.

She stretched luxuriously, feeling as if her skin was smiling— as if her entire being had undergone some new dawn—and laughed softly to herself as she recalled precisely how that had been achieved.

But found herself wondering at the same time how Daniel had managed to free himself from the sensuous tangle of arms and legs that had entwined them, get dressed and go—all without waking her.

Well—years of practice was probably the unwelcome answer to that question, she thought, biting her lip. As she sat up, she glanced casually at the radio-alarm, and stifled a yelp when she saw it was nearly ten o clock—which made her horrifically late for work.

As she threw back the covers she noticed the folded sheet of paper propped against the lamp.

Its message was brief.

Darling, I've told your company you won't be in today. I
have meetings this morning, but I'll be free for lunch—so
let's make it the Savoy at one-thirty. There's something I
need to tell you.

It was simply signed with his initial.

As a love letter, it had its flaws, Laine thought wryly as she read
it again. But then who was to say that's what it was? She refolded
the paper slowly, aware that her heart was thudding unevenly.
Because, in spite of everything that had happened between them
last night, the word 'love' hadn't been mentioned once.

And it would be unwise to read too much into a lunch date
which might just turn out to be a substitute for a bunch of flowers.
If that was what men did after they'd slept with you. She wasn't
even certain about that.

In fact, she couldn't really be sure about anything. But maybe
she could hope—just a little.

So, what did you wear to lunch at the Savoy with your lover?
she asked herself, after she'd showered and washed her hair, and
stood in her prettiest underwear, riffling along her clothes rail.
At the end, shrouded in a plastic cover, she found the yellow dress
that she'd worn to begin her honeymoon. He once wanted to take
it off, she recalled with a sudden giggle, and when lunch is over
and we come back here then I'll encourage him to do exactly
that—button by button. And see when his patience runs out.

She left early for their date, and caught a bus to the West End,
the sun warm on her face as she wandered along, scanning the
shop windows with eyes that saw little. For one thing this kind
of browsing had never really appealed to her. For another she had
begun to wonder what Daniel needed to discuss with her—and
in such a public place too. Surely, if there was something he
needed to say, he could have woken her this morning and said it?

Deep in thought, she almost collided with someone emerging
from a shop, stepping aside with a murmured apology, only to
hear a girl's voice say, 'Excuse me—but isn't it Laine—Laine

Sinclair?' And realised, to her horror, she was confronting a smiling Belinda.

'How nice to run into you again,' she was saying. 'Have you got the morning off? Because I was just thinking of having a drink break. Why don't you join me?'

For more reasons than you can possibly imagine, Laine thought grimly, discovering she was being ushered irresistibly towards a neighbouring coffee shop.

In a city of all these millions, why have I bumped into you— the last person in the world I want to see or have to think about?

Yet she should have considered Belinda, she acknowledged miserably as they found a table and studied the menu. Should have let it register that she might be poaching on the other girl's preserves. But she hadn't given her a thought—not then—not since—and maybe being made to sit with Belinda now and smile and make conversation was a kind of instant karma.

Because if you hadn't been involved with Daniel I think I could have liked you, she reflected miserably. We might even have become friends—done the whole shopping, coffee-drinking thing as a matter of course.

And I wouldn't be feeling so damned guilty…

When the waiter came she ordered a cappuccino she didn't want, while Belinda chose herbal tea again.

'I shall be so sick of the stuff before I'm finished,' she sighed, then eyed the small gold-striped bag Laine had placed on the table. 'Have you been buying something lovely?'

Laine touched it defensively. 'Just some of my favourite scent.' *The one I wore in bed last night.* 'Although I can't really afford it any more,' she added with constraint.

'I've worn the same perfume all my life too, and now I suddenly can't bear the smell of it. Isn't that weird?'

Laine shrugged. 'Perhaps you're just tired of it?'

'Maybe,' Belinda agreed as their drinks arrived. 'Or perhaps it's something else.' She leaned forward. 'Oh, goodness, I do realise we hardly know each other, but even so I've got to talk about it or I'll burst. You see—I'm pregnant. That's why I've sworn off coffee for the duration—because I'm having a baby.'

There was an odd roaring in Laine's ears, and she suddenly seemed to be looking at Belinda through the wrong end of a telescope.

A voice she recognised as hers said with perfect normality, even pleased interest, 'But that's wonderful. Congratulations.'

Belinda sighed happily. 'It is great. Completely unplanned, of course, but I couldn't be more thrilled.'

There's something I need to tell you.

Oh, Daniel—*Daniel*…

She looked at Belinda's ringless hands. 'And your—partner must be delighted too.'

'Well, his initial reaction left a lot to be desired.' The other girl pulled a face. 'But obviously we hadn't meant it to happen—or not yet—and it was a shock.' She grinned. 'But he's grovelled suitably, and decided to become very excited about the whole thing, so I've decided to forgive him.' She looked dreamy. 'And I know he'll make a wonderful father. I mean—you must know who it is.'

'Yes,' Laine said, with a calmness that astonished her. 'Of course.' Under its froth, her cappuccino tasted as bitter as gall. If she drank it she'd be sick—so sick. Maybe she could get sick enough to die, and then she would never have to think again of Belinda having Daniel's baby. Of Daniel and Belinda together—married—settled. Family. 'He—he'll be marvellous with children.'

Last night, she thought, agony searing her. How could last night possibly have happened when he knew—all this?

Because she'd thrown herself at him. That was the how and the why. Because he'd chosen to be kind, not to humiliate her with a direct refusal. Because he could spare her the last gift of one night.

For, in the long term, it made no real difference to his plans. And that was what he intended to tell her over a very public lunch at the Savoy. A place where she could be trusted to behave well and not make a scene loaded with recriminations.

And at least he'd been honest enough not to pretend that he

loved her. There might come a time when she'd be grateful for that. But not now…

Belinda was still chattering gaily. 'Of course they can tell you in advance what sex the baby is, but I'm not sure I want to know. Would you?'

'I—I'm not sure. Probably not.' Laine pushed her cup away, her stomach revolting. She glanced at her watch and gave an elaborate start.

'Heavens—is that the time? My shift will be starting, so you'll have to excuse me, I'm afraid.'

'Oh.' Belinda was disappointed. 'Do you have to go?' She hesitated. 'I hope I'm not driving you away—rabbiting on like this about the baby?'

'Absolutely not.' Laine put down some money and got up, offering a taut smile which was almost a grimace. 'It was so nice to see you again. And I wish you—all the best for the future. You—and your man.'

Somehow she made it outside again, wandering along blindly with no idea where she was going. A girl in a yellow dress on a sunny day with nothing inside her but darkness—and the knowledge that her heart was breaking.

CHAPTER ELEVEN

SHE wanted to vanish. To simply disappear and not be heard from again—much as she'd intended when she went off to Florida. But that hadn't worked them, and it would succeed no better this time, because it was the coward's way out. Besides, she had nowhere to go.

Instead, she went back to the flat, changed into her uniform, leaving the yellow dress on the floor, and went to work.

'I thought you had a virus.' Denise was surprised to see her.

'A passing thing.' She shrugged. 'And soon gone.'

But when the day was over she would have to return to face him. To put an end to it and let him go, salvaging what little remained of her pride on the way. She had no other choice.

Because, if she was honest, she had no one to blame but herself for what had happened. The annulment of their marriage had set Daniel free to pursue other relationships, and if he was going to find happiness with Belinda she'd forfeited any right to stand in his way.

And if she'd allowed her desires and emotions to overrule her common sense and decency, then that was her problem.

In a way, what had happened between them was the setting of unfinished business from two years ago. A kind of closure. Which was how she had to regard it, no matter what her feelings might be.

Because nothing could be worse than sitting across at table

in an expensive restaurant, listening to Daniel trying to tell her gently that their relationship had no future. And why.

He must never know that she'd hoped—even for a moment—that things might be different, that they might have had a chance of happiness together.

So once again, it was up to her to walk away.

And as she cleaned and polished, quickly and mindlessly, she came up with the beginnings of a plan.

He was there at the flat before her, standing by the fireplace, his jacket and briefcase flung on one of the sofas, and as she hesitated by the door he raised his head and looked at her.

'You didn't come to the Savoy,' he said quietly. 'Why?'

'I left a message,' she said quickly. 'Didn't they give it to you?'

'I learned you wouldn't be meeting me. Now I'm waiting for an explanation.'

'I couldn't get away,' she said. 'I can't take unnecessary time off. I need to earn my living, therefore I have to—prioritise.'

'And evidently I don't come high on your list?' He paused. 'Which means, presumably, that last night made no difference.'

She lifted her chin. 'What do you want me to say? That you more than lived up to your—considerable reputation? That you're amazing in bed—a revelation—the standard by which all future lovers will be judged? Well, yes. All that and more. I freely admit it.

'But.' She shrugged quite deliberately. 'But—it was a one-night stand, and we both know it, so it would be silly to attach any more importance to it than that.'

'A one-night stand?' Daniel repeated slowly.

'Well, please don't pretend that you've never heard of them—or not had your fair share.' There was danger in the room, she could feel it, but she pressed on, forcing a smile. 'Dan, I'm grown-up now. I know how these things work.'

'Then perhaps you'd enlighten me,' he said. 'Because I thought last night was a beginning, not an end.'

She thought of Belinda's shining eyes. Oh, Dan, how can you say that—how can you? You have another beginning—another commitment now. And she needs you—needs your loyalty...

She wanted to scream at him, to hurl accusations, to call him a liar—all kinds of a bastard—but knew it was not the way. That she had to stick to her guns in order to survive. Therefore, 'How could it be?' she drawled. 'Shall I be frank? As you said, we've come to the parting of the ways, and I confess I'd always wondered, rather shamefully, what it would be like to go to bed—to lose my virginity—with someone who really knew what he was doing, and this seemed to be my final opportunity.'

She paused. 'And now my curiosity is satisfied. End of story.'

'Surely more than just your curiosity, my sweet?' he said silkily. 'If memory serves.'

'Why, yes,' she said. 'But that doesn't mean I require a repeat performance.'

How can I be doing this? she asked herself, pain twisting inside her. *How can I be reducing to vulgar triviality all that beauty and passion and sweetness that I discovered in his arms? His gentleness with me that first time—the way he coaxed me to rapture? How can this possibly be happening?*

He took a step towards her. His voice was harsh. 'But if I wish to refresh my memory—what then?'

'Then I'd fight,' she said. 'And that would make it rape.'

'Dear God,' he whispered, and turned away.

His back to her, he said, 'I asked you to the Savoy to talk. Aren't you remotely interested in what I wanted to say?'

She bent her head. 'Whatever it was, it makes no difference. Because it's none of my business. We're both—moving on. Our lives are going to take us down different paths. I can accept that, so why can't you?'

'Because that's not the whole truth, Laine.' He swung round, his face like stone. 'You were going to meet me. I know you were. Because when I got your message I came here to find you. It suddenly occurred to me, you see, that after last night you might be too shy to face me in daylight in a crowded restaurant.'

He threw back his head. 'And in your room I found a dress on the floor. A dress that I remembered. Something you'd clearly intended to wear, then changed your mind. And I need to know why.'

She said, 'Because last night was—last night. And that's all it was. It can never be anything else. And this time I managed to change my mind before I made another terrible mistake.'

'You don't consider your virgin sacrifice to have been some kind of error?' His voice bit. 'That it should have been a privilege for the man you love?'

She flinched inwardly. 'The man I love isn't around any more. And I drove him away.' She looked down at the floor, afraid to meet his gaze in case he saw the truth in her eyes. Realised she was talking about him. 'And he won't be coming back,' she added expressionlessly. 'So—staying celibate under those circumstances seemed a little pointless.'

He said, too quietly, 'Are you telling me that, in spite of everything, you still—care for him?'

'I'm telling you we can't choose who we love. And perhaps I've discovered that I'm a one man girl, and that sex, however, fantastic, is not going to change that.'

The silence between them was ice, and it seemed to stretch out to eternity.

At last he said, 'I see,' then picked up his jacket and briefcase and headed for his room.

Laine came away from the door, aware that her legs were shaking under her. She felt grimy, inside and out, but her ploy seemed to have worked. And she'd done it without mentioning Belinda, or his impending fatherhood, or anything might else which might cause her to fall apart in front of him.

When Dan returned he'd changed, and was carrying a travel bag, along with his briefcase and laptop.

He said curtly, 'I'm taking only what I need for tonight. I'll arrange to have the rest of my stuff picked up tomorrow.'

'Where are you going?' The question escaped before she could stop it, and it was stupid—stupid—because she already knew the answer.

He was already at the door, but he turned back to look at her, the bitterness in his eyes searing her skin like acid.

He said softly, 'Give me a break, Laine. What do you care?' And went.

'You're losing weight,' said Denise. 'Go on like this, you'll have to ask Mrs M for a smaller overall.' She paused. 'How do you manage it?'

'It's simple,' Laine returned lightly. *You simply arrange to be agonisingly, unbearably unhappy.* 'I just watch what I eat.' *Watch it, push it round the plate, then throw it away. Oh, and I sleep badly too. It all works a treat.*

But it had forced her into a decision about the flat. Jamie and Sandra seemed settled in New York. They were talking about marriage, and clearly had no plans to return, so selling up and splitting the money suddenly made a lot of sense.

Besides, since Daniel had left, three weeks ago, the place had become unendurable. Even stripped of his possessions—and the firm he'd used had been thorough in the extreme—everything about it managed somehow to remind her of him, and how much she'd loved him. How much she loved him still, she corrected herself bitterly. She couldn't even move back into her own bedroom. It was far too painful—too redolent of memories that tormented her day and night.

She was almost scared to pick up a newspaper in case it mentioned him, or carried a report—pictures—of his wedding.

So, best to put the flat on the market, achieve the best possible price, and make a fresh start. Perhaps belatedly undergo some form of training for a proper career, instead of simply drifting from day to day because she was too heartsick and weary to make real decisions about her life.

And one day she might even be glad to open her eyes in the morning.

When they reported back at the office, Mrs Moss greeted Laine unsmilingly. 'A young man left this for you.' She handed over an envelope. 'We're not a dating agency, you know.'

Laine said levelly, 'I assure you I've never given that impression to anyone.' She took the envelope, opened it, and scanned the brief typewritten lines.

We need to meet again and talk.
I'll be at Blakes Bistro in Jurgen Street tonight from eight p.m. Please be there too.

It was unsigned.

She turned to Mrs Moss. 'Did he leave a name?' she asked urgently.

The older woman shook her head. 'Just said to make sure you got it.' She snorted. 'I told him he had some nerve.'

'Well, what did he look like?' Laine persisted. *Daniel—it has to be Daniel. No one else knows where I work. But why, suddenly, after nearly a month of total silence?*

'Didn't notice.' Mrs Moss thought for a moment. 'Good-looking, I suppose, if you like that kind of thing.'

Denise dug Laine in the ribs. 'Got yourself a secret admirer, have you?'

'No admirers at all,' Laine said wearily. 'As far as I know.'

'Might be the bloke in number eleven,' Denise offered helpfully. 'He looked as if he could have the hots for you.'

In spite of her inner turmoil, Laine shuddered. 'Thanks.'

'And any fraternisation with clients is strictly against the rules.' Mrs Moss added her sharp two-pennorth.

'I'm relieved to hear it,' Laine said grimly, and went home with the note burning a hole in her bag and not the least idea how to deal with it.

She spent the next hour pacing around, confusion and panic

fighting a war inside her. Asking herself what harm it could do to see him again—just once. Then remembering that 'just once' was a taboo phrase in her vocabulary. Knowing that she should tear up the note and burn its fragments. Telling herself it was futile and damaging to speculate why he'd asked to see her again.

And that she was not under any circumstances obliged to go to this meeting.

Told herself again as she pressed the yellow dress, wondering if it would be third time lucky, and found the dark green jacket that topped it.

Even when she was actually walking in through the bistro's glass door, she was still silently repeating the same valuable advice. Reminding herself it was not too late to turn back and walk away.

And then a waiter was advancing, asking her name, offering to take her jacket and requesting her to follow him to the booth in the corner.

'Miss Sinclair is here, sir,' he reported, and faded away as Laine saw with total incredulity exactly who was waiting to greet her.

'Hello, sweet thing,' said Andy. He looked bronzed and fit, showing his teeth in the warm, honest smile she remembered only too well. He added airily, 'Good to see you again.'

Shock mixed with an agony of disappointment had turned her legs to jelly, so it was either sit down or fall down, and she opted to subside onto the high-backed bench on the opposite side of the table.

'You,' she said blankly, then, on a rising note of anger. '*You?* I don't believe it.'

'I thought this might be a bit tricky,' he said. 'That's why I didn't sign the invitation.' There was a bottle of red wine on the table, and two glasses. He filled the empty one and pushed it towards her. 'Have a drink. You look as if you need it.'

She ignored it. 'What the hell do you want?'

'You don't seem too pleased to see me,' he remarked. 'Not really what I was led to expect, but there you go.'

'Pleased?' Laine stared at him as if he'd grown two heads. 'When you took my money and abandoned me to that—subhuman scumbag.' She took a deep uneven breath. 'I could have been raped and—dumped. Did you ever think of that?'

He shrugged. 'You know the old saying—girl with skirt up runs faster than man with trousers down. My money was on you, Laine.'

'*Our* money,' she said. 'I think you'll find.'

'Talking of which.' He reached inside his jacket and handed her a folded piece of paper.

She took it unwillingly. 'What is this?'

'It's a bank draft,' he said. 'For your share of the boat. I didn't think you'd trust my personal cheque.'

She stared down at the printed figures. 'My God,' she said shakily.

'So,' he said. 'We're square.' He leaned forward, lowering his voice. 'Laine, I didn't mean to leave you stranded. I swear it. But I was in a spot of bother, and really needed to be elsewhere fast.'

'How strange,' she said. 'I had a similar experience around the same time.' She tucked the draft in her bag. 'And elsewhere seems to be renewing its appeal right now, so I'll wish you good evening.'

'Laine.' His voice was husky with appeal. 'Don't go. You have every right to be furious, but I'm trying to make amends here. I'm back on my feet now, and looking for something new to invest in—especially if I can find a partner. After all, we made a damned good team before, and this time we might do even better.' The blue eyes looked into hers directly. Winningly. 'Get— closer, maybe? End up as real partners, just as I always wanted. So, how about it? What do you say?'

'Nothing,' she said, 'that I'd care to speak out loud in a re-spectable restaurant.' She shook her head. 'Andy, I was a fool to trust you, I don't think I ever liked you, and I wouldn't have you served up with truffles. That's the polite version, and I hope it's clear enough.'

'Oh, yeah.' The charm gave way to a sneer. 'But I had to ask, so I did. It was part of the deal. And now that you've turned me down, do me one last favour? Tell your boyfriend to get his heavies off my back.'

'Boyfriend?' Laine repeated slowly. 'I don't know what you're talking about.'

'Your publishing tycoon and his band of private detectives.' His face was scowling, his tone sullen. 'Do you really think I'd have repaid you a cent if they hadn't tracked me down and leant on me? Asking bloody questions, looking into past deals, threatening me with the FBI and worse.' He gave a short, angry laugh. 'Best of all, he actually claimed you fancied me, and that you might be prepared to forgive and forget if approached in the right spirit. Boy, did the bastard get *that* wrong.'

He gave her an insolent look. 'Pity, really. I was quite flattered at the idea you'd been secretly pining for my body all along. Wouldn't have minded at all taking you back to my hotel and teaching you a thing or two in bed—even if you have become a bit skinny for my personal taste.'

His eyes narrowed. 'And even though I strongly suspect you're not nearly as naïve as you were. Your millionaire pal get there first, did he?' He grinned unpleasantly. 'Poor little Laine. You can't have made much of an impression if he was so eager to hand you on.

'Now I'll be on my way. Look for more appealing company myself.' He got to his feet. 'But don't leave on my account. Celebrate your windfall, finish the wine.' He paused. 'And, as you're the trash with the cash, I'm sticking you with the bill. Hope you don't mind. Have a great evening.'

She didn't even watch him leave. She leaned back against the wooden panels behind her and closed her eyes, her mind whirling as she tried to absorb what he'd said. *Your publishing tycoon.*

Daniel had done this—for her. Traced Andy, the man he thought she loved, and made him compensate her. Even suggested a reunion might be possible because she'd told him so. And he'd actually believed her. Believed that ridiculous story.

He'd gone to all that trouble, she thought. But why?

Because maybe it might make him feel less guilty about sleeping with her and betraying Belinda? About having his own life to go to when she would be alone?

Or because he still felt a sense of obligation to the burden that Simon had bequeathed to him?

I wanted to set him free, she thought. And I've failed even in that.

She signalled to the waiter, paid the bill and walked out to the bar area while she waited for her jacket. And felt a hand touch her arm.

'Laine?' someone said. 'Laine, we saw you come in and your—friend leave. Are you all right?'

She turned, found herself looking at Belinda's concerned, pretty face and wanted to die.

Oh, God, she thought. Daniel must be here watching, making sure the reconciliation is complete and that the course of true love runs smooth this time. Which would be almost funny if it wasn't so nauseating.

She pulled herself together. 'Everything's fine. He's someone I used to know, and we—we simply discovered we had nothing in common any more.'

'Poor you.' Belinda's sympathy was genuine. 'But don't just push off, please. My husband's over there, and we'd love you to join us.'

The hand on Laine's arm was wearing a ring—a plain circle of gold.

So it has happened, Laine thought, and somehow I missed it.

'No,' she said. 'Really, I couldn't.'

'But why not?' Belinda coaxed. 'After all, you know each other. You're not strangers.'

And that's why, Laine wanted to shriek at her. That's why I can't do the polite social thing. Why I can't sit with your lover and remember when he was my lover too. Why I can't laugh and talk, eat and drink, as if it didn't matter.

'I have to go,' she said. The waiter arrived with her jacket, and she took it thankfully. 'Another time, perhaps?'

'At least stop and say hello,' Belinda urged.

Her stomach was churning, but she forced a smile. 'Well, just for a moment.'

She followed Belinda across the room to another booth, screened by a large pot plant on a stand—which explained why she hadn't noticed their presence earlier. And, of course, the shock of her confrontation with Andy.

And soon—soon—this living nightmare would be over, and she could go home.

The plant's leaves brushed her jacket as she walked past it, bracing herself as she prepared to meet Belinda's husband, who was rising courteously but warily to greet her. And saw a stocky man with brown hair, and a face that was pleasant rather than handsome. A man she'd last seen two and a half years ago, at her wedding reception flirting with Celia.

And she thought, My God, it's Daniel's best man.

Aloud, she said uncertainly, 'Guy—Guy Lawson? *You're* Belinda's husband?' She shook her hand. 'I don't understand.'

'What's to understand?' His blue eyes were cold.

Her mouth was dry. 'I thought she was married to Daniel.'

They both stared at her. 'But you couldn't,' Belinda said at last. 'Not possibly.'

'You were there at the flat. You'd spent the night.' Laine clapped her hands to her mouth, looking at Guy in horror. 'Oh, God, I—I mean—'

'Listen,' said Belinda. 'Dan found me limping along in the rain, because I'd broken the heel on my shoe, raving with temper because I'd just had a flaming row with Guy over dinner and walked out on him, leaving my bag on the table in the restaurant—ergo, no keys and no money.'

She spread her hands. 'So—he rescued me, which is one of the things he's so great at. Dragged me into his cab and, when I refused point-blank to go home, took me back to his place, where he sat me down and gave me a good talking-to. Explained how easy it was to let love slip away and spend the rest of your life with regret.

'Then he lent me his bed for the rest of the night, while he slept on the sofa. In the meantime, of course, while I was in the bathroom, he quietly phoned Guy, advised him to let me simmer down and pick me up in the morning. Which is exactly what happened.'

She made another helpless gesture. 'But surely you *knew* this? Did you never ask Dan what was going on—why I was there?'

'Of course not,' Guy said scornfully. 'When has she ever given a damn about what's happening in his life? I was one of the poor devils who had to try and put him together again when she dumped him on their honeymoon. And even after that he's still been there for her.' He shook his head. 'Unbelievable.'

'Guy,' Belinda said in reproach.

'It's time someone told her.' He looked back at Laine, his face implacable. 'You didn't want him, so why didn't you let him off the hook? Go away and stay away. But, no, you had to come back, and now you're driving him out instead.'

'I don't know what you're talking about.'

'He's relocating to the States. Selling that damned barn of a house he's been slaving over—everything—and moving out. Yes, America's always been the main base for the company, but his home has always been—*here*. England's the place he's always returned to. And now that's all going to change permanently. We're losing him.'

'And you blame *me* for this?' Laine, reeling from the hammer-blows of his words, squared her shoulders, facing him bitterly. 'Because I needed more from our marriage than Dan could give me? Because I wanted to be loved as a woman, not as another rescue case—like some stray kitten saved from drowning, who just needs a good home to make her happy? Is that—really—so terrible?'

'Loved?' Guy almost spat the word. 'Good God, woman, he was crazy about you—head over heels in love with you. What more did you want?'

She shook her head. 'No, it wasn't like that. You don't understand. You don't know.' She stopped, realising she was on the verge of saying the unsayable, betraying her deepest secret. Suddenly she couldn't think straight. Didn't know what she was doing any more, because Dan was leaving. Dan was going away for ever.

Her throat closed with the pain of it. She muttered, 'I'm ruining your evening. I'd better go.' She tried to smile at Belinda. 'I hope everything turns out wonderfully for you.'

'Laine.' Belinda came after her into the street, her face pale and anxious. 'Please don't leave like this. I'm so sorry. Guy didn't mean to upset you, but he thinks the world of Daniel—we all do. And he was shocked when he found out from me that you were living together. Up to then I knew nothing about Dan having been married, or how it had turned out. It was just—never mentioned.'

No, Laine thought sadly, as she turned away after a hug and a word of reassurance. Never mentioned—like so many things. And now it's too late. So very much too late. And somehow I must learn to live with that.

CHAPTER TWELVE

SHE felt bone-weary as she emerged from the lift and crossed to her flat. She fitted the key into the lock and tried to turn it, but nothing happened. For some reason, her door was unlocked already.

Oh, God, she groaned inwardly, now I've been burgled. The perfect end to an already bloody evening.

She opened the door cautiously and peeped in, then stopped, aware that her jaw was dropping. Because the intruder was still there, on the sofa, his jacket and tie discarded, his shirt unbuttoned. There was an open bottle of Scotch on the table in front of him, and a half-filled glass in one hand.

'Daniel.' She almost whispered his name, as if saying it aloud would make him somehow disappear. She came fully into the room and closed the door behind her. 'What are you doing here?'

He said slowly, staring at the whisky in his glass, 'I needed a place where I could think undisturbed. This suggested itself.'

'But how did you get in?' She took off her jacket. Laid it across the back of a chair. 'Your removal men gave back the key.'

'Jamie's key,' he said. 'I still had my own.'

She looked at the bottle, and then at him. 'You came here to drink?'

'Not just drink,' he said. 'To get blasted—totally and completely destroyed. Obliterated.' He held up the glass to the light, examining its contents with a frown. 'They used this as anaesthetic in the old days. Drink enough of it on some battlefield and they could amputate a limb, apparently, without you feeling a thing. I was planning to see if that was true. If it can really blot out that kind of pain.'

He put the glass down. 'But my experiment will have to wait, because here you are, and you want your flat back. I apologise for my intrusion.'

She said, 'What kind of pain?'

'There are many levels,' he said. 'But principally the kind that comes from thinking of you with another man. Letting him kiss you—touch you—as I once did.'

She took a step nearer. 'But I'm not with another man.'

'No.' He glanced at her, still frowning, assessing what she was wearing. 'Why is that, may one ask?' He added sardonically, 'After all, you went on your date dressed to be undressed.'

'We decided we weren't suited.' She sat on the sofa opposite, putting her bag beside her. 'However, the evening wasn't totally wasted.' She produced the bank draft. 'This is for a lot of money.'

'So I should hope.'

'And it must have cost you a great deal in time and expense to get it for me.' She paused. 'You didn't even know his full name.'

'Jamie did.'

'Ah,' she said. 'Those mysterious phone calls. I didn't think of that.' She looked down at the draft. 'Anyway, some of this should be yours.'

'I won't hear of it.' He hesitated. 'If you want to repay me in some way, you could ditch that dead-end job and do something good with your life.'

She glanced coolly at him and saw him wince.

'I'm sorry,' he said. 'It's none of my business.'

'But I've always been your business, Daniel, whether you wanted it or not.'

His mouth tightened. 'I'm also sorry things didn't work out for you in—other ways.'

'Ah.' She gave a faint shrug. 'But, as I once said, you can't choose who you love.'

'But how much easier it would be if we could.' There was bitterness in his voice. 'Think of it, Laine. Just—tick a box and the job's done. None of this hanging round waiting for a look—a smile. Counting the hours until you see her again. Dreaming of the night when you'll hold her in your arms at last.'

She looked down at her hands, clasped together in her lap. 'I thought you'd ticked a box labelled Belinda.'

He sat up, his face incredulous. 'Are you crazy?'

'I found her here a few weeks back, wandering round in nothing but one of your shirts. I—I thought she was your girl-friend. Then I saw her again, when I was on my way to meet you, and she told me she was pregnant. I assumed you were the father, and thought it would be best if I—faded out of the picture.'

'I think our definitions of "faded" might differ.' His face was expressionless. 'In effect, I laid my life at your feet a second time, only to have it kicked away again.'

'But she was at the bistro tonight—with her husband. They—put me right about a few things.'

'How brave of them. But does it ever occur to you that I could have done the same—if you'd asked?'

'Perhaps I was afraid to ask.'

'Scared of me?' Daniel shook his head. 'I find that hard to believe.'

'Scared of the answers I might get.' She hesitated. 'And of you—a little.'

'Ah, well,' he said. 'It really doesn't matter any more. As you also said once—we've come to the parting of the ways. I suppose Guy and Bel told you I was leaving England?'

'Yes. Isn't that a little drastic?'

'Perhaps. But sometimes you have to give up dreaming and face reality.'

'Through the bottom of a glass? Some reality.'

'And that,' he said gently, 'is none of *your* business.' He reached for his jacket. 'Now, I'll take my anaesthetic and go.'

'Not yet, please. There's something I need to ask you.' She swallowed. 'What did you want to say—that day at the Savoy?'

'Nothing that has any relevance.'

She took a deep breath. 'I wondered if you were going to tell me that you—loved me. That could be terribly relevant.'

'You've never found it so in the past,' he said, his tone almost matter-of-fact. 'But—for the record—I've loved you all my life, but I fell in love with you on your seventeenth birthday, when you trembled as I kissed you. And I realised I was trembling too.'

'Oh, God—why—why didn't you tell me?' There was anguish in her voice.

'Because I was ashamed of myself. For one thing, you were far too young for that kind of commitment, and I told myself you should finish your education—have a career—live a little. For another, I suspected if Simon knew what I was thinking he'd want to kill me.' He paused. 'And how right I was.'

She said slowly, 'But Simon *wanted* you to marry me.'

'The hell he did. We had the worst fight of our lives over it. Nearly came to blows.'

Laine was gasping. 'But how—why?'

He shrugged. 'Because in Simon's eyes you were still his baby sister, in need of protection, and I could keep my filthy hands off you.'

'But he asked you to be responsible for me—if anything happened.'

'Yes, but strictly on his own terms.' His mouth twisted wryly. 'I was to become surrogate brother, guardian and friend, but nothing else. As he made all too clear, whatever I might wish, I was never going to be in the running as husband or lover. Because you were a young and innocent child, and I was the exact and disgusting opposite.'

'But you were his best friend…'

'And as such he didn't have many illusions about me.' He paused. 'Anyway, how do you know he asked me to look after you?'

Laine met his gaze, her face white. 'You wrote him a letter agreeing, but saying it wasn't what you wanted. That I was a burden you didn't need, and it could wreck both our lives.' She bit her lip. 'Candida found it among Simon's things, and gave it to me just before we left on honeymoon.'

'Candida,' Daniel said reflectively. 'That poisonous bitch. Simon was finishing with her, you know, before he set off on his trip. No doubt she blamed me for that, although I swear I never said a word against her while they were together. But he'd begun to see for himself that all that blonde beauty was only skin-deep. That there was a mean, nasty little soul underneath. Showing you my letter would have been her way of getting her own back.'

'But I was grateful to her at the time,' she said in a low voice. 'Because it—it implied that you were only marrying me out of pity—for Simon's sake—and I couldn't bear it. Couldn't endure the thought of you—touching me—making love to me—out of kindness. Couldn't live that kind of lie.'

'Dear God, Laine,' he said huskily. 'I wanted you more than life itself. Could hardly keep my hands off you. How did you not know that?'

'But you never said anything—did anything to show how you felt…'

'I didn't dare. Because you were still too young, and in my heart I knew it.'

He paused. 'Laine, I'd never intended to rush you into marriage so soon. I'd anticipated that Simon would come back safely, and that you and I could enjoy a long and leisurely courtship in which to get you used to the whole idea—and maybe, because I was no saint, introduce you to several new ones.

'Then I discovered you were being dragged off to Spain, and suddenly there was no time to lose any more.'

'But even after you asked me to marry you—you didn't…'

He came to sit beside her, taking her hands in his. 'Darling,' he said gently. 'I knew that sex was a closed book to you, and therefore it would be fatally easy to open it at the wrong page and maybe ruin everything. Anyway, I thought you would feel safer—happier—if you were my wife when I took you to bed for the first time.

'Also, I was concerned about the kind of reaction you'd get at home if we became lovers,' he added grimly. 'Because both your mother and Candida would have picked up on it instantly, and no doubt commented, and I didn't want you exposed to that kind of malice.'

He paused. 'Besides, if we're really being honest, I was scared too.'

'Scared?' Laine repeated. 'You? I don't believe it.'

'It happens to be true. I'd never been in love before, and it made me feel—vulnerable. And you didn't give me much encouragement, my love. So I began to worry that it might not be just shyness. That in fact you might not actually want me. After all, you'd never said that you loved me, and I wasn't even sure you really knew what marriage would mean. Not just the sex thing, but the entire business of sharing our lives.'

'But you never said you loved me either,' she whispered. 'Not even that night when we…'

'Darling, I said it each time I touched you. And I was saying it before—whenever I looked at you—every time you came into the room. On our wedding day I thought my heart would burst with all that I felt for you. Then I watched you go upstairs to change, my laughing eager girl, only to come down a stranger who wouldn't speak or meet my eyes. And I didn't know why. Only that my worst nightmare seemed to be coming true, and I didn't know how to deal with it.'

'But that letter to Simon. It made you sound so totally unwilling…'

'I can understand that it might have,' he agreed. 'Taken out of context. Besides, I was actually agreeing to spend the foreseeable future being a brother to you when my feelings couldn't have been less fraternal, so my reluctance was understandable. But what you didn't see, my darling, was Simon's reply, which I still have, and which I will show you one day. In it, he said he'd been doing some hard thinking too, and realised he'd no right to say the things he had, or to make those kind of demands about what form my care of you should take.

'That he was so completely used to considering you as a child it had never occurred to him that you were growing into a woman I could love and want as my wife. And that it would be entirely wrong to block my desire to woo you because, on reflection, he now suspected it was what you wanted too, and he'd just ignored the signs.

'So, I was off the hook. Free to love you and look after you in the way that I wanted. He added that if we could control ourselves until his return, he'd give you away at our wedding.'

'If only he had,' she whispered. 'If only he had.'

'I've wished it too,' he said. 'With every day that's passed. But he's given us to each other now, I think. Hasn't he?'

'Yes,' Laine said on a little sigh. 'Oh, yes.' She paused. 'Dan, I once said I'd never stolen from you, but it wasn't true. Because I stole two years when we could have been making each other happy.'

'How very true,' he said, smiling at her. 'I shall have to make sure you get ample opportunity to make it up to me for the rest of our lives.' He added, more seriously, 'Until death us do part, my dearest love. I'll settle for nothing less.'

He picked her up and put her on his lap, holding her close, kissing her as he whispered all the things she'd longed to hear him say, then kissing her again.

'But you should have told me the truth, darling.' He stroked her cheek as they paused for breath. 'Let me know what was troubling you.'

'I dared not,' she said ruefully. 'Suppose you'd admitted that it was all true? I couldn't have borne that, and yet I had no guarantee that wouldn't happen—and not even much hope either.'

'And I was left with no hope at all. Just hurt, anger and bitterness.'

He sighed. 'I told myself I'd get over it. That I'd adjust to having a life you were no longer a part of. But, no matter how hard I tried, it didn't happen. I realised you were the only wife I would ever want, and that I had to get you back—however long it took, and by whatever means. Also, that I'd been a bloody fool to walk away without fighting for you.

'And when I found you'd gone—disappeared to Florida with that bastard—I nearly went mad. I was going to follow you down there—snatch you off that damned boat if need be. Then I calmed down and realised that you might genuinely be in love with the swine, and that I should play a waiting game, however hard that was.

'In the meantime, I moved in here. Living in your flat, sleeping in your bed was a poor second-best, but it was all I could do to get close to you. At the same time I realised that I might need something else to offer you, along with my hand and my heart. Some kind of extra inducement to persuade you to try again.

'Then, when you came back hating me, I knew it was going to be an uphill struggle, and I was going to need every atom of patience and self-control I possessed.'

'I—didn't make it easy for you,' Laine said, nestling against him.

'No, my darling, you didn't. Even when we finally became lovers I wasn't sure of you. So, after lunch at the Savoy, I planned to put you in the car and drive you down to see your wedding present. It wasn't finished, of course, but I was going to say, This is the home you once said you wanted. A place for a family, where children can grow up and be happy, as we once were. Because that's true, isn't it, darling? Not all the memories are bad ones?'

'Abbotsbrook!' Laine sat up, staring at him, lips parted. 'Oh, my God—you bought Abbotsbrook.' Her voice broke. 'That—that's the house you've been renovating, isn't it? You bought it for us?'

He nodded. 'Yes, and it was one hell of an act of faith, as I had no guarantee that I'd ever get you back. And it's also occurred to me since that you might hate the idea, so I want you to know that it doesn't have to happen. That we can find another house entirely if that's what you'd prefer.'

'No, no.' She was climbing all over him, laughing and crying at the same time, kissing every bit of him she could reach. 'I think it's a wonderful—wonderful idea. Oh, darling—darling! When can I see it? Can we go now?'

'We could.' He pulled her back into his arms and began to unfasten the little yellow buttons, slowly and with immense care. 'But I do have other plans for the immediate future, which you might find just as interesting.'

'Oh,' Laine said, with a little gasp, as his hand slid inside her dress. 'Well—tomorrow would be fine. Or the next day.'

'Or even,' Dan said softly, 'the day after that.' And he began to kiss her.

HARLEQUIN *Presents*

Men who can't be tamed...or so they think!

If you love strong, commanding men,
you'll love this brand-new miniseries.

Meet the guy who breaks the rules to get exactly
what he wants, because he is...

HARD-EDGED & HANDSOME
He's the man who's impossible to resist....

RICH & RAKISH
He's got everything—and needs nobody...
until he meets one woman....

He's RUTHLESS!
In his pursuit of passion; in his world the winner takes all!

Coming in November:

THE BILLIONAIRE'S CAPTIVE BRIDE
by Emma Darcy
Book #2676

Coming in December:

BEDDED, OR WEDDED?
by Julia James
Book #2684

Brought to you by your favorite Harlequin Presents authors!

www.eHarlequin.com
HP12676

HARLEQUIN *Presents*

THE ROYAL HOUSE OF NIROLI

Always passionate, always proud.

**The richest royal family in the world—
a family united by blood and passion,
torn apart by deceit and desire.**

By royal decree, Harlequin Presents is delighted to bring you
THE ROYAL HOUSE OF NIROLI. Step into the glamorous,
enticing world of the Nirolian royal family. As the king ails,
he must find an heir. Each month an exciting new installment
follows the epic search for the true Nirolian king.

Eight heirs, eight romances, eight fantastic stories!

Available November

EXPECTING HIS ROYAL BABY

by Susan Stephens

Book #2675

Carrie has been in love with Nico Fierezza for years. After
one night of loving, he discarded her...now she's carrying
his child! Carrie will do anything to protect the future of
her baby—including marrying Nico?

Be sure not to miss any of the passion!

Coming in December:

THE PRINCE'S FORBIDDEN VIRGIN by Robyn Donald

Book #2683

www.eHarlequin.com

HPI2675

HARLEQUIN® *Presents*®

INNOCENT MISTRESS, VIRGIN WIFE

Wedded and bedded for the very first time

Classic romances from your favorite Presents authors

Available this month:

THE SPANISH DUKE'S VIRGIN BRIDE
by Chantelle Shaw
#2679

Ruthless billionaire Duke Javier Herrera needs a wife to inherit the family business. Grace is the daughter of a man who's conned Javier, and in this he sees an opportunity for revenge and a convenient wife....

Coming soon,
THE DEMETRIOS BRIDAL BARGAIN
by Kim Lawrence
Book #2686

www.eHarlequin.com

HP12679

REQUEST YOUR FREE BOOKS!

2 FREE NOVELS
PLUS 2
FREE GIFTS!

YES! Please send me 2 FREE Harlequin Presents® novels and my 2 FREE gifts. After receiving them, if I don't wish to receive any more books, I can return the shipping statement marked "cancel." If I don't cancel, I will receive 6 brand-new novels every month and be billed just $3.80 per book in the U.S., or $4.47 per book in Canada, plus 25¢ shipping and handling per book and applicable taxes, if any*. That's a savings of close to 15% off the cover price! I understand that accepting the 2 free books and gifts places me under no obligation to buy anything. I can always return a shipment and cancel at any time. Even if I never buy another book from Harlequin, the two free books and gifts are mine to keep forever.

106 HDN EEXK 306 HDN EEXV

Name _____ (PLEASE PRINT) _____

Address _____ Apt. # _____

City _____ State/Prov. _____ Zip/Postal Code _____

Signature (if under 18, a parent or guardian must sign)

Mail to the **Harlequin Reader Service®:**
IN U.S.A.: P.O. Box 1867, Buffalo, NY 14240-1867
IN CANADA: P.O. Box 609, Fort Erie, Ontario L2A 5X3

Not valid to current Harlequin Presents subscribers.

Want to try two free books from another line?
Call 1-800-873-8635 or visit www.morefreebooks.com.

* Terms and prices subject to change without notice. NY residents add applicable sales tax. Canadian residents will be charged applicable provincial taxes and GST. This offer is limited to one order per household. All orders subject to approval. Credit or debit balances in a customer's account(s) may be offset by any other outstanding balance owed by or to the customer. Please allow 4 to 6 weeks for delivery.

Your Privacy: Harlequin is committed to protecting your privacy. Our Privacy Policy is available online at www.eHarlequin.com or upon request from the Reader Service. From time to time we make our lists of customers available to reputable firms who may have a product or service of interest to you. If you would prefer we not share your name and address, please check here. ☐

HP07

HARLEQUIN *Presents*®

Enjoy two exciting,
festive stories to put you
in a holiday mood!

THE BOSS'S
CHRISTMAS BABY
by Trish Morey
Book #2678

Tegan Fielding is supposed to be masquerading for
her twin, not sleeping with her sister's boss! But how
will sexy James Maverick react when he discovers his
convenient mistress is expecting the boss's baby?

JED HUNTER'S
RELUCTANT BRIDE
by Susanne James
Book #2682

It's Christmastime when wealthy Jed Hunter offers
Cryssie a job, and she's forced to take it. Soon Jed
demands Cryssie marry him—it makes good business
sense. But Cryssie's feelings run deeper....

Available November wherever you buy books.

www.eHarlequin.com

HPCM1107

HARLEQUIN®

Mediterranean
NIGHTS™

---

*Not everything is above board
on Alexandra's Dream!*

*Enjoy plenty of secrets, drama and sensuality
in the latest from Mediterranean Nights.*

Coming in November 2007...

BELOW DECK

by

Dorien Kelly

Determined to protect her young son,
widow Mei Lin Wang keeps him hidden
aboard *Alexandra's Dream* under cover of
her job. But life gets extremely complicated
when the ship's security officer, Gideon Dayan,
is piqued by the mystery surrounding this
beautiful, haunted woman....

www.eHarlequin.com   HM38965

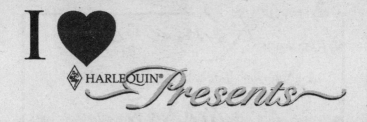

I ♥ HARLEQUIN® *Presents*

**BROUGHT TO YOU BY FANS OF
HARLEQUIN PRESENTS.**

We are its editors and authors
and biggest fans—and we'd
love to hear from YOU!

**Subscribe today to our online blog at
www.iheartpresents.com**

HPBLOG

HARLEQUIN
Romance.

New York Times bestselling author

DIANA PALMER

Handsome, eligible ranch owner Stuart York knew
Ivy Conley was too young for him, so he closed his heart
to her and sent her away—despite the fireworks between
them. Now, years later, Ivy is determined not to be
treated like a little girl anymore…but for some reason,
Stuart is always fighting her battles for her. And safe in
Stuart's arms makes Ivy feel like a woman…his woman.

Winter Roses

Available November.

www.eHarlequin.com

HRIBC03985